HEARTBREAKER

Cara Walker stretched out on the sand beside Jessica. "Looks like Bill Chase is striking out for greener pastures," she said, smirking.

Jessica frowned. "Doesn't DeeDee ever give up?"

"I don't know," Elizabeth observed. "It looks like Bill is having a pretty good time."

But he's in love with me, not DeeDee, Jessica thought. DeeDee wasn't half as pretty as she was. Was Bill really losing interest in her?

Impossible!

Abruptly, Jessica stood up and yanked off her sun visor. She shook her hair so that it tumbled over her shoulders, and set off down the beach with a saucy step. She added a slight swing to her hips, for the benefit of Bill Chase.

She smiled. If DeeDee thought she was any match for the Wakefield magic, she had another think coming.

Bantam Books in the Sweet Valley High Series
Ask your bookseller for the books you have missed

#1 DOUBLE LOVE
#2 SECRETS
#3 PLAYING WITH FIRE
#4 POWER PLAY
#5 ALL NIGHT LONG
#6 DANGEROUS LOVE
#7 DEAR SISTER
#8 HEARTBREAKER
#9 LOVE ON THE RUN
#10 WRONG KIND OF GIRL

SWEET VALLEY HIGH

HEARTBREAKER

Written by
Kate William

Created by
FRANCINE PASCAL

BANTAM BOOKS
TORONTO • NEW YORK • LONDON • SYDNEY • AUCKLAND

RL 7, IL age 12 and up

HEARTBREAKER
A Bantam Book / May 1984

Sweet Valley High is a trademark of Francine Pascal

Conceived by Francine Pascal

*Produced by Cloverdale Press Inc.,
133 Fifth Avenue, New York, N.Y. 10003*

Cover art by James Mathewuse

ISBN 0-553-24045-5

Published simultaneously in the United States and Canada

Bantam Books are published by Bantam Books, Inc. Its trademark, consisting of the words "Bantam Books" and the portrayal of a rooster, is Registered in U.S. Patent and Trademark Office and in other countries. Marca Registrada. Bantam Books, Inc., 666 Fifth Avenue, New York, New York 10103.

PRINTED IN THE UNITED STATES OF AMERICA

O 0 9 8 7 6 5 4 3

To Marian Woodruff

One

"Kiss me," Jessica purred seductively in Bill's ear. "Maybe we can get it right this time."

Color flooded Bill Chase's tanned cheeks, turning them a dull brick red. Jessica knew he was really squirming. It was only a rehearsal for the drama club's spring play, but to Bill it was obviously all too real. Poor Bill, she thought, suppressing a wicked smile. He was madly in love with her. It was too good an opportunity to let pass.

They'd rehearsed this scene, the big love scene from *Splendor in the Grass*, at least a dozen times already. Each time Bill kissed her, Jessica insisted it wasn't right—forcing him to do it again despite his embarrassment.

"OK, I'll try," he mumbled.

Bill leaned close, squeezing his eyes shut so he wouldn't have to look at Jessica. Even so, he could still see her—those deep, deep blue-green eyes, the spun-gold hair that drifted silkily about her shoulders, her cameo of a face, perfect down to the adorable dimple that showed up in one cheek when she was smiling.

As Bill's lips hovered inches from her own, Jessica only half tried to stifle the giggle that erupted out of nowhere. Bill's eyes flew open. His face turned from dull red to crimson.

"Sorry, Bill," Jessica twittered. "I just couldn't help it. You looked so funny, all puckered up like that."

A ripple of laughter passed through the onlookers. Mr. Jaworski, the drama coach, was the only one who wasn't amused.

"I think we can call it a day," he announced dryly. "Let's all meet here same time tomorrow. And don't worry, Bill," he added, looping an arm about his leading man's shoulders, "you're doing just fine. Just relax and don't take everything so seriously."

"Sure, Bill," Jessica put in, shooting him a dazzling grin. "You did your best. It's not your fault that kissing me is such a deadly chore."

"I don't mind. I—I like kissing you," Bill stammered, then quickly hung his head, his thick blond hair fanning over his forehead, when he realized what he'd just said.

Well, it was only fair, Jessica thought. Once upon a time, she'd asked him to a Sadie Hawkins dance, and he'd done the unforgivable—he'd turned her down. Jessica never forgot an insult, especially one as serious as someone refusing the golden opportunity to go out with her. Bill Chase was only getting what he so richly deserved.

She'd been waiting for an opportunity to get back at him, and several weeks ago the perfect one had finally come along. It was during the period when her identical twin sister Elizabeth was behaving so strangely after a motorcycle accident she'd been in, and had accepted dates with two different boys on the same night. By the time Bill Chase showed up, Elizabeth was long gone with Bruce Patman. Jessica quickly stepped in, pretending to be Elizabeth. While she had Bill duped into thinking she was Elizabeth, Jessica turned on her charm full force. Bill never stood a chance. By the time he discovered the deception, it was too late. He was hopelessly hooked on Jessica.

"That was really mean, Jess."

Elizabeth cornered her twin in the hallway after the rehearsal and forced Jessica to meet her gaze. It was like looking into a mirror. The two girls were identical in every way—the same honey-and-sunshine hair, the same aquamarine eyes and perfect, even features—except that Elizabeth's face wore a concerned expression in contrast to Jessica's look of playful triumph.

"You know Bill's crazy about you," Elizabeth went on. "Did you have to rub his nose in it?"

Jessica shrugged. "I was only teasing him. I kid around with a lot of people."

"With Bill it's different, and you know it."

"Can I help it if he's in love with me?"

"Come on, Jess, that's like the spider telling the fly it's his fault for getting stuck in the web."

"Are you implying I'm responsible?" asked Jessica, fluttering her long lashes in complete innocence. "Remember, Liz, I only went out with him in the first place to save your skin. *You* were out with Bruce, if I recall."

Elizabeth groaned. "Ugh, don't remind me!"

Normally, Elizabeth would never have agreed to go out with Bruce Patman. That he was handsome, popular, and rich didn't change the fact that Bruce was a stuck-up creep, in her opinion. The trouble was, she hadn't been her normal self the night she'd gone to his beach house.

Jessica linked an affectionate arm through her sister's. "Not that I'm blaming you, Liz. I know you couldn't help it. After all, Bruce is so disgustingly ugly and unpopular, anyone would have *had* to be crazy to go out with him, right?"

Elizabeth wasn't sure how Jessica managed it, but somehow Elizabeth always found herself being defensive when it was her sister who was in the wrong.

She sighed. "Bill's not like Bruce. He's nice, and he really likes you."

"I know, I know," Jessica gloated. "It's a real problem, isn't it?"

The truth was, she was enjoying every bit of it. Bill was actually kind of cute in a cool, mysterious way, and certainly not unpopular, though not many people had gotten close to him. He was a loner who lived to surf—sort of a mystery man. Falling in love with Jessica had probably been more of a surprise to Bill himself than to anyone else. He obviously wasn't used to being out of control and didn't know how to handle it. Half the time he spent gazing at her with a moonstruck expression, the other half he spent avoiding her like the plague.

"Maybe for Bill it's a problem," Elizabeth agreed. "For you, I'm sure it's just one more broken heart to add to your list. Just be careful what you do to him."

"I don't know what you're talking about. I'm not *doing* anything."

"That's just the point. If you're not going to go out with him, stop leading him on."

Jessica giggled. "That might be kind of hard, since I already *am* his leading lady."

"Sure, Jess. I know it's all a big joke to you. Just don't get carried away, OK?"

"Anything you say, big sister." Elizabeth was older only by four minutes, but sometimes it seemed more like four years.

"Listen," Elizabeth said. "I've got to go now. I only came by to meet Todd here. Bill's elected him as a sort of unofficial cheerleader." Elizabeth's boyfriend, Todd, was the closest thing Bill had to a good friend.

"Bill's really uptight about this play, isn't he?" Jessica asked.

"Can you blame him? It's the first time he's ever gotten involved in anything like this. He's usually too busy surfing."

"Blame it on Mr. Collins. I heard he was so impressed by Bill's reading of *Macbeth* in English class that he practically forced Bill to try out for the play."

"Well, I'm glad he did," Elizabeth said. "I think Bill is really talented. Although," she added with a laugh, "I don't think he'll win an Academy Award for kissing you."

"Oh, my God, Liz, speaking of kissing . . ." Jessica leaned toward her sister, lowering her voice to a whisper. "Looks like you've got competition." She darted a look over her shoulder.

Elizabeth followed her glance, barely managing to stifle a horrified gasp. Standing beside Todd was one of the most beautiful girls Elizabeth had ever seen—and he had his arms around her! Elizabeth felt as if the bottom had dropped out of her stomach. Slowly, stiffly, she made her way toward them.

"Oh, hi, Liz!" Todd disengaged himself from Miss America's arms as he greeted Elizabeth.

"Listen, I want you to meet an old friend of mine. Patsy Webber."

Elizabeth stuck out a hand that was as limp as a rag in comparison to Patsy's cool, confident grasp. "Hi," Elizabeth croaked. If Patsy was such a good friend, why hadn't she heard of her before?

"Nice to meet you, Liz."

Patsy smiled, revealing glorious white teeth and a charming dimple in her heart-shaped chin. *She could be a model!* Elizabeth couldn't help thinking. Patsy looked too sophisticated to be in high school. She was wearing a straw-slim skirt belted with a wide leather sash around her tiny waist, and delicate high heels. Her coppery-red hair was cut fashionably short in back, with a tumble of curls that dipped over her forehead. A pair of slanted green eyes regarded Elizabeth with friendly interest.

Immediately Elizabeth felt guilty for suspecting the worst. Patsy was probably very nice, she told herself. Why shouldn't Todd hug her if she was an old friend? That was all there was to it. She was stupid to be jealous.

"Patsy's been living in Paris," Todd explained. "Her father was transferred over there at the end of her freshman year."

Patsy sighed. "Dad's always getting transferred. Sometimes I feel like a Ping-Pong ball. But this time we're home to stay. I hope," she added with a giggle.

"Home?" Elizabeth echoed.

"Sweet Valley now. I'll be going to school here. We used to live in Palisades." Impulsively Patsy threw her arms around Todd once more. "You can't imagine how good it is to be back in the area. To see all my old friends."

She was gazing up at Todd with an expression that seemed to hint at something far more than friendship. Todd looked pleased by all the attention, as well as faintly embarrassed.

"Patsy seems nice," Elizabeth told Todd when Patsy had moved out of earshot and was talking to someone else. Elizabeth bit her lip. "Were you two very good friends?"

Todd slipped an arm about Elizabeth's shoulders. She looked up at him, marveling for the hundred thousandth time that he was hers. Tall, muscular, with wavy brown hair and velvety brown eyes, Todd was easily one of the cutest boys in Sweet Valley High. He was also the basketball team's hottest star.

Todd cleared his throat and looked away. "Actually, Liz, I used to go out with Patsy. But that was way before I met you, so don't worry. We're just friends now."

"I'm not worried," Elizabeth said quickly. It was partly true. She trusted Todd, she really did. He had stuck by her during that awful time after the motorcycle accident. The least she could do was give him the benefit of the doubt now.

It was just that Patsy seemed so different

and special. It probably came from living in Paris. Dressed in comfortable old jeans and a tank top, Elizabeth felt dull and uninteresting in comparison. She was sure Todd had noticed as well.

Bill and one of the other cast members, DeeDee Gordon, joined them, and they began walking down the hall together.

"You were great, Bill," Todd reassured his friend. "Didn't you think so, Liz?"

Elizabeth nodded enthusiastically.

"Fantastic!" DeeDee chimed. She was small and athletic-looking, with a roundish face dusted lightly with freckles and merry brown eyes that peered out from a glossy dark fringe of bangs.

Bill was staring at the floor as he walked, his hands shoved into the pockets of his baggy cords. He shook his head slowly. "I don't know. Sometimes I really like this play. But other times I'm sorry Mr. Collins talked me into it. I—I just don't know if I'm right for the part."

"You're just saying that because Jessica gave you such a hard time today," Todd said. "Don't let her bug you. She just likes to get a rise out of people."

Bill flushed at the mention of Jessica. Quickly he jumped to her defense. "It's not Jessica's fault. It's mine. I just don't know if I'm good enough."

"Of course you are!" DeeDee bristled. Her role was only a minor one, so she spent plenty of time watching Bill. It was obvious that she thought he was terrific. "You're a natural, Bill," she went on. "That's what makes you so good. It's like you're not even acting. You're just being yourself." Realizing she was gushing, she stopped, her cheeks growing warm.

Bill looked at her, his blue eyes round with incredulity. "You really think so?"

"Listen to DeeDee," Elizabeth put in. "She ought to know. Her father's a hotshot Hollywood agent."

DeeDee blushed. "I usually don't like to tell people. They might wonder what he's doing with such an untalented daughter."

Now it was Bill's turn to defend DeeDee. "What makes you say that? I happen to think you're pretty good."

She shrugged. "So-so. But it's like everything I do. Take surfing, for instance. When you're out there on your board, it looks so easy. Right now, I'm trying to learn, and I feel like King Kong."

"You probably just need someone to give you a few tips." Bill's whole face lit up; he was in his element when discussing surfing. "I'll be glad to help you the next time you're down at the beach."

DeeDee smiled shyly. "Would you really? I mean, it wouldn't be too much trouble? Oh, Bill, that would be terrific!"

Elizabeth and Todd exchanged a knowing look.

"No trouble at—" Bill stopped dead in his tracks as he spotted a familiar figure at the far end of the corridor.

Jessica was deep in conversation with Tom McKay, her arm linked cozily through his. Tom looked tanned and gorgeous in his white tennis shorts and polo shirt. Jessica spotted their group and waved. As they passed by her, she shot Bill a coy look and blew him a kiss.

Bill looked as if he'd just been knighted by the queen of England. He stood there for a long, hypnotized moment—a huge grin plastered across his features. Then, just as suddenly, it was gone, and he darted away in red-faced embarrassment.

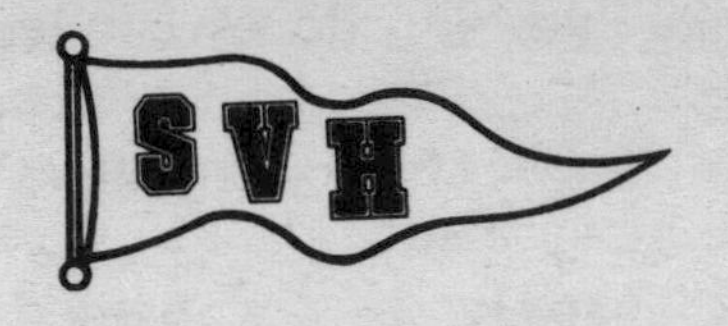

Two

"It's not fair!" Jessica wailed. "I always get stuck with the dishes."

Mrs. Wakefield smiled. "That's funny—I could've sworn it was Liz who took your turn the last two times."

"But I've got a date at seven-thirty. I'll never be ready in time."

"Seems like I've heard that argument before," Mr. Wakefield said, taking a sip of his coffee. "Sorry, Jess, but it would never hold up in court." The twins' father could seldom resist bringing his lawyer's logic into play.

Elizabeth sighed as she rose from the table and scooped up a stack of dishes. "This could go on all night. C'mon, Jess, I'll help you. I wouldn't want Tom to be robbed of a single precious moment of your company."

Jessica flashed her sister a grateful look. "Thanks, Liz, I owe you one."

"That's what you *always* say. Honestly, Jess, if I ever started collecting on all those I-owe-you-one's, you'd probably be my slave for the rest of your life."

"Yes, master." Jessica giggled and bowed to Elizabeth with a flourish. "Your wish is my command."

"In that case, I command you into the kitchen. I said I'd *help,* but I don't want to get stuck doing it all."

Elizabeth, trying to look stern, waved a long serving fork at Jessica, who shrieked and hurried ahead of her into the kitchen.

Sighing, Alice Wakefield settled back to finish her coffee. With her sunny blond good looks, it was easy to see whom the twins resembled, though she looked youthful enough to be their older sister.

"Whoever said trouble comes in threes obviously didn't have twins," she observed, chuckling.

In the spacious, Spanish-tiled kitchen, Elizabeth and Jessica's antics quickly escalated to a full-fledged soap-suds war. Elizabeth had filled the sink with soapy water to wash the pots, while Jessica loaded the dishwasher. As soon as Jessica's back was turned, Elizabeth scooped up a handful of suds and let fly. Not to be outdone, Jessica retaliated with a soapy volley of her own—an attack that left both Elizabeth and the floor drenched.

"See what you made me do?" Jessica gasped when her laughter had subsided. "Now I'll never be finished in time!"

"I hope Tom knows how to swim," Elizabeth joked as she handed her sister a mop.

"Funny. Very funny." A look of mischief crossed Jessica's lovely face. "You know something? We ought to get Bill to clean it up. He's the one who's so crazy about water."

Instantly Elizabeth sobered. "Poor Bill. You never let up, do you? He'd probably swim to Tahiti if you asked him to."

"What good would he do me in Tahiti?" Jessica snickered. "He's much more useful to me right here."

"As your go-fer, you mean?"

"You said it, not me."

"Come on, Jess, enough is enough. Why don't you give Bill a break? He's really a nice guy. What did he do that was terrible enough to earn the fate of falling in love with you?"

"Nothing, that's what." Her eyes narrowed. "He's only getting what he deserves for ignoring me in the beginning."

"Since when is turning you down for a date a federal crime?"

Jessica grew defensive. "I can't help it if Bill is crazy about me, can I? I mean, I'm not exactly holding a gun to his head."

"Maybe not," Elizabeth observed, "but the way you tease him is just as lethal." She thought of something, and a slow smile spread across her face. "I have a feeling he'll soon be put out of his misery, though."

Jessica frowned. "What are you talking about?"

"I'm talking about DeeDee Gordon." Elizabeth went back to scrubbing the broiler pan. "Looks like she's got her eye on Bill."

"*That* little nobody?" Jessica sneered. "Anyway, why should I care? I don't even like Bill."

"Then I guess you won't care that he volunteered to give DeeDee surfing lessons."

"He *what*?" Jessica exploded. "He can't do that!"

"Why not?"

"He just can't, that's all," Jessica muttered sulkily. "He, uh, he won't have time. What about rehearsals? He's got an obligation to the drama club." Abruptly she shoved the mop at Elizabeth. "That reminds me—I've got to call him. I forgot my script. I'm sure he won't mind lending me his."

"But I thought you were going out!" Elizabeth called after her in frustration. "Hey, wait a minute, you're not finished!"

Jessica turned to flash her an appreciative grin. "You don't mind, do you, Lizzie? It's just a teeny little puddle. I'd be eternally grateful, and I'll pay you back—you know I will."

"Teeny little puddle?" Elizabeth cried. "It looks like Marine World in here!"

"I've got to rush. You're a doll, Liz. I won't forget this!" With a wave, Jessica vanished.

"Neither will I," Elizabeth grumbled through clenched teeth as she attacked the kitchen floor with the mop.

An hour later Elizabeth was immersed in her homework when the doorbell rang. Jessica was out, and their parents had gone to a movie, so Elizabeth ran downstairs to see who it was. Somehow she wasn't surprised to see Bill standing there.

"Oh, hi, Liz." He hastily put on a smile, trying not to look disappointed. "Where's Jessica? I brought over the script she wanted. I—I was hoping we could maybe study our lines together."

He stood in the doorway, looking uncomfortable as he shifted from one foot to the other, hands shoved into his front pockets. As he shuffled inside, Elizabeth saw the rolled-up script sticking out of his back pocket.

What was she going to tell Bill? She felt herself flushing. Darn Jessica! She hated it when her sister put her on the spot like this.

"Jessica's not here," she explained, biting her lip. "Uh, something came up at the last minute, and she couldn't wait. I'm really sorry, Bill." Elizabeth couldn't bring herself to meet his disappointed gaze. In a rush of sympathy, she added, "But, look, now that you're here, why don't you sit down for a minute? I'll get you something to drink."

Bill shrugged as he slumped in the nearest chair. Elizabeth had a feeling she could have served him arsenic at that moment and he wouldn't have cared. She ducked into the kitchen, returning a minute later with two lukewarm cans of root beer. It had been Jessica's turn to put away the groceries last time, and she'd stuck the soft drinks into a cupboard instead of the refrigerator.

Bill didn't seem to notice. "I guess it must have been something pretty important, huh?" he asked, not sounding too terribly convinced.

"I'm sure it was."

A look of pain crossed Bill's tanned face. "Probably a date with another guy, right?" he said softly. It wasn't a question so much as a statement.

"Bill, I—" Elizabeth didn't know what to say. She felt so sorry for Bill, she could have cheerfully strangled her sister at that moment.

"It's OK, Liz, you don't have to explain. I—I kind of expected it anyway. I mean, Jessica's so beautiful, she probably has a million guys after her."

"I can't think of anyone who would be nicer than you," Elizabeth offered kindly. "But—but I'm not really sure Jessica is right for you, Bill."

Bill flushed a mottled red. "What do you mean?"

Now she was really stuck. She'd just wanted to help Bill, to make him see he didn't stand a chance with Jessica, but it was obvious she'd only managed to make things worse. How could she tell Bill how hopeless it was without being disloyal to her sister?

"I—well, you know Jessica. It's practically impossible to pin her down in one place for more than five seconds. I don't see how *anyone* could keep up with her."

"Yeah, she really is something, isn't she?" Bill's face glowed with adoration.

"That's one way of describing her."

"I can't blame her if I'm not the only one who sees it," he said, forcing a weak smile. "I guess I'll just have to get used to standing in line, huh?"

"Bill, I don't think—"

He stood up, leaving his root beer untouched.

"Thanks, Liz, but I really should get going. I have a pile of homework."

"Why didn't you tell Jessica you had homework when she called?" Elizabeth scolded gently.

"Yeah, well," he muttered sheepishly, "when she called, I sort of forgot everything else."

Bill's blindness where her sister was concerned reminded Elizabeth of an animal paralyzed by the headlights of an oncoming car. If he didn't watch out, he was going to get squashed flat, she thought. Only deference to Jessica kept her from telling him so.

After Bill had gone, Elizabeth was depressed. She needed to talk to Todd. He was Bill's friend—maybe *he* could make Bill see that loving Jessica was as futile as trying to bail out a leaky rowboat. But when she called, Todd's mother told her he wasn't home.

"Do you know when he'll be back?" Elizabeth asked.

"I'm not sure, dear," Mrs. Wilkins answered. "He didn't say where he was going." She sounded vaguely sympathetic, which left Elizabeth to wonder why Todd's mother should feel sorry for her.

Then a wave of panic swept over her as a sudden image of Patsy Webber rose in her mind. She pictured Todd with his arms around her. Patsy was tall—with high heels she was just the right height to gaze into Todd's eyes without getting a crick in her neck the way Elizabeth sometimes did. She imagined Todd leaning toward Patsy, eyes closed, lips parted. . . .

"Stop it!" she commanded herself out loud.

There were times when her writer's imagination ran so wild that she actually found herself getting upset about things that hadn't even happened. Todd was probably out with one of his friends, she told herself. Or he could be practicing basketball or studying at the library.

He didn't have to inform her of his whereabouts every waking minute, did he?

Even so, Elizabeth couldn't shake the worry she felt. What if Todd really *was* out with Patsy?

In that case, Bill would have to move over to make room for two in his leaky rowboat, she thought miserably.

Three

Bill swallowed hard against the knot forming in his throat. *OK, so she stood you up. What did you expect?* Jessica was so beautiful. With a million guys chasing after her, why should she pick him? Still, he couldn't erase her bright image from his mind. *Just go home and forget about it,* he told himself as he drove slowly down the quiet street.

But before he realized what he was doing, Bill had turned onto the coast highway instead. Fifteen minutes later he was coaxing his battered old VW bus over a bumpy dirt road leading to the beach.

It was deserted when he arrived. A full moon cast a ghostly light over the waves that crowded into shore, and the sand gleamed silver. Bill crouched at the foot of a dune. He scooped up a handful of cold sand, letting it trickle slowly through his fingers. He was remembering another time . . . another girl. It had been so long, and the memory was so painful. He tried to shut it out. But he couldn't do it, couldn't stop the memories from coming any more than he could stop the tears that were rolling down his cheeks.

Her name was Julianne. He had gone out with her when he was living in Santa Monica, before his parents got divorced and he and his mother moved to Sweet Valley. They were freshmen when they met. They had seats next to each other in math class, but they were too shy to strike up a conversation.

That didn't stop Bill from looking at her any chance he got, though. She was so beautiful. She had long blond hair that seemed to dance with sparks of light when the morning sun shone on it. Her eyes were bluer than blue, so deep they were almost purple. When she smiled, they crinkled up at the corners. He would stare at her and completely lose track of what the teacher was saying.

Then one day he was out surfing when a slim figure in a wet suit cut across in front of him.

"Hey, watch it!" he yelled in annoyance. Then he saw who it was. Julianne! She was the last person in the world he would have expected to see out there.

He paddled over to greet her. "You're pretty

good," he told her. "Where did you learn to surf like that?"

She laughed. "I was practically born in the water. My parents have a house just down the beach. I've been surfing since I was five. You're pretty good yourself. I've been watching you for a while."

"Why didn't you tell me?"

"I was afraid it would make you nervous," she replied, blushing. "Besides, you're not exactly the talkative type." Not even her embarrassment could hide the teasing sparkle in her eyes.

Now it was Bill's turn to blush. "I guess I couldn't think of anything to talk about before."

"Well, we have something in common now," she said and smiled.

"We do? Uh—what?" Bill stammered, so flustered he couldn't think straight.

"Surfing!"

They both laughed. After that, Bill found conversation easy. It turned out they had more than surfing in common. He discovered she loved the same books and music he did. They were both crazy about old movies and monster comics and Mexican food. Julianne was an only child, too, so she knew what it was like to be a loner.

They spent the rest of the afternoon chasing waves, zigzagging in front of each other, showing off their best moves. At sundown they paddled in, then gathered up a pile of driftwood and built a huge bonfire. They sat in front of it, holding hands and talking, until they were toasted dry. It seemed to Bill as if they'd known one another for years. When he kissed her, it was as natural as a wave breaking.

After that, they were inseparable. Bill grew to love her more with each passing day. They shared everything. When Julianne's beloved old cocker spaniel had to be put to sleep, it was Bill who accompanied her to the veterinarian's and dried her tears afterward. When Bill broke his leg the day before the big spring dance their sophomore year, Julianne chose to stay home with him rather than go alone.

Sure, they'd had their fights. Mostly just silly little arguments, but they could never stay mad at each other for long. Bill would never forget the fight they'd had the night of Sue Cuthbertson's party, though. He'd accused Julianne of flirting with Eddie Roth. It probably wasn't true. Later on, he realized that he had just been jealous because he knew how much Eddie liked her. Julianne was so upset that she left the party without Bill, grabbing a ride home with a friend. The second she walked out the door, Bill realized how foolish he'd been. He made up his mind to call her as soon as she got home.

He never got the chance because Julianne never reached her house. It was raining. The car she'd been riding in slid out of control on a slick curve and exploded against an embankment. Julianne was killed instantly.

For Bill it was like the end of the world. He went a little crazy the night she died. Blinded by guilt and anguish, he grabbed his surfboard and took off for the beach, plunging into the storm-tossed waves. The tide was so strong he was swept out to sea and would have drowned if a coast guard cutter hadn't spotted him in time. They brought him home semiconscious, muttering Julianne's name over and over.

Afterward, he developed pneumonia, but he was too brokenhearted to care whether he got better or not. What was the use of living without Julianne? How could he go on, knowing he'd never see her again? What made it even worse was that he felt responsible for her death. If only he hadn't started that stupid argument! If only he'd insisted on driving her home himself!

Slowly, as the days passed and he recovered, Bill began the painful process of inching his way out of the black tunnel of his grief. Julianne would have wanted him to live, he realized. She would have wanted him to remember their love with joy, not sorrow. She was too forgiving a person to have blamed him for what had happened.

Still, it wasn't easy. There were days when he couldn't bear the thought of not seeing her sweet, smiling face. He dreamed of her almost every night. Gradually, though, the ache diminished.

The move to Sweet Valley was a new beginning in many ways, but he still found it hard to be around other girls. He'd be talking to a girl, and suddenly he'd be seeing Julianne's face, hearing her laughter. Blinded by tears, he would have to turn and walk away.

The first time he saw Elizabeth Wakefield he was stunned by the resemblance to Julianne. The same shimmering blond hair, the same deep blue eyes. He got goose bumps every time he looked at her. But that was right after he'd arrived in Sweet Valley. He still wasn't completely ready to let go of Julianne's memory—that was why he'd turned Jessica down that time she'd asked him out. He was scared stiff of falling in love again—and getting hurt. Jessica, like her twin, reminded him too much of Julianne.

Now it was too late, he told himself miserably. Whatever whim had attracted her to him in the first place was a thing of the past.

Bill noticed that it was getting cold. He shivered in his thin T-shirt. The wind had dried his tears. Time to head back. Ever since the time he'd almost drowned, his mother worried about him when he stayed out too late.

He stared up at the moon, and for an instant his vision blurred, and he saw a face that could have been either Julianne's or Jessica's. He blinked, and it was gone.

Bill trudged back to his car. Maybe he'd never find love again. Maybe some people were just doomed as far as love was concerned. . . .

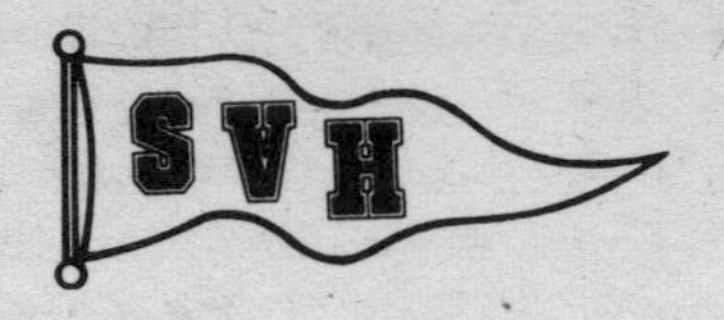

Four

"Hey, Jess, looks like Bill is striking out for greener pastures," Cara said, smirking. "Or should I say greener *waters*?"

Cara Walker stretched out on the sand beside Jessica, her dark hair and olive complexion a striking contrast to her best friend's blond good looks. It was a glorious day at the beach, and half the student body of Sweet Valley High was lazily taking advantage of it. And no one seemed to be enjoying it more than Bill Chase, whose name was practically synonymous with sun and surf. At the moment he was engaged in giving DeeDee surfing lessons.

Jessica frowned as she watched them. "Doesn't DeeDee ever give up?"

Cara snickered. "Maybe she lassoed him with a piece of seaweed."

"I don't know," Elizabeth observed. "Looks to me like Bill is having a pretty good time."

She sat up, brushing the sand from her legs. "Would you please pass me the suntan lotion?"

Jessica lobbed it at her sister as if it were a hand grenade. What did Elizabeth know? *Bill is in love with me, not DeeDee,* Jessica assured herself.

"Looks like Liz is right," Cara said. "But maybe they're just practicing for the play. Only they're calling it *Splendor in the Surf.*"

"You're a real riot, Cara," Jessica said, only she wasn't laughing.

"You have to admit one thing, Jess," Elizabeth remarked. "DeeDee does look pretty good for a beginner."

Of course, Jessica would never have admitted such a thing out loud, but secretly she had to agree with her sister. As Jessica watched, a glassy swell rolled in with DeeDee riding it. Though she didn't dance over the board with the ease of the more experienced surfers, at least she managed to stay on. It was obvious she was a natural, and with a little more practice she could be really good. Straddling the board in an eye-catching canary-yellow one-piece, she even managed to look alluring enough to make Jessica a little bit nervous. Still, DeeDee wasn't half as pretty as she was. Why was Bill wasting his time?

"Bill tells me he's been giving her lessons every day after school," Todd put in.

He was in the midst of rubbing suntan

lotion on Elizabeth's back. He paused to kiss the nape of her neck as he lifted her hair.

"Yeah, Bill's a real sweetheart," Jessica cracked, but inside she was fuming. Suppose Bill really was losing interest in her?

Impossible!

Abruptly she stood up, yanking off the sun visor she wore. She shook her hair so that it tumbled over her shoulders. "I think I'll go swimming," she announced.

Cara squinted up at her. "I thought you didn't want to get your hair wet."

"Well, I changed my mind," Jessica tossed back defiantly, ignoring the warning glare Elizabeth shot her.

Determinedly she set off down the beach. Aware of the stares she was getting in her bronze, wet-look bikini, she added a slight swing to her hips, for the benefit of her male audience. One boy dove in front of her to retrieve his Frisbee. "Pardon me, gorgeous," he muttered, flashing her a grin of apology.

Jessica smiled. If DeeDee thought she was any match for the Wakefield magic, she had another think coming.

"Hi, there!" Jessica sang out as she splashed her way through the swirling foam toward Bill. "I didn't know you gave surfing lessons."

"Not really," he said. "I'm just giving DeeDee a few tips."

"How sweet. Maybe you wouldn't mind giving me a few sometime. I've always wanted to learn how to surf."

"S-sure, Jessica," Bill stammered. "Anytime. I'd—I'd like to."

With a sinking heart, DeeDee watched the transformation in Bill. A minute before, he'd been relaxed and confident, chatting easily with her as he showed her how to crouch low on the end of the board to gain the maximum speed. Jessica's appearance was like a wave knocking him over. All of a sudden he seemed to have trouble catching his breath.

"Let me know when you have the time," Jessica said. "It looks as if you're pretty busy right now. I wouldn't dream of interrupting." She started to turn away.

"You're not interrupting," he threw out in desperation. He shot a look at DeeDee that pleaded with her to understand. "Maybe I could teach both of you at the same time. You—you could use my board, Jessica."

DeeDee's face felt tight and hot. For some reason she felt like crying. But that was crazy, wasn't it? She and Bill were just friends.

She forced a smile for Bill's sake. She knew he'd rather be alone with Jessica but was too polite to say so to her face.

"Oh, that's too sweet of you, Bill," Jessica

drawled. "But I really do hate to butt in. You know what they say, two's company, three's a crowd. Maybe some other time."

Bill looked so stricken that DeeDee couldn't stand it any longer. "Don't rush off on my account," she said with forced brightness. "I was just going in anyhow. I've been in the water so long that I'm starting to shrivel up."

Jessica wrinkled her nose in distaste. "Gee, that's too bad, DeeDee. Mind if I use your board?"

"Go ahead." DeeDee was fighting back her tears as she turned to Bill. "Thanks. I really learned a lot today. You're a good teacher."

But Bill wasn't looking at her. He was focused on Jessica as if hypnotized. "Uh, sure, DeeDee. You were great, too. Keep up the good work."

As DeeDee trudged up through the backwash, a silvery peal of laughter rippled out over the water. She could hear Jessica declare breathily, "Oh, Bill, it'll take me a hundred and thirty-seven *years* to learn all this. . . ."

"A little to the left, Bill. I think you missed a spot on my shoulder." Jessica languished on her beach towel while Bill, her adoring slave, rubbed suntan lotion on her back.

Elizabeth looked on in disgust. How could Jessica be so obvious? She looked as smug as the cat who's just eaten the canary. Only in this case the victim was a girl in a canary-yellow bathing suit. Farther down the beach, DeeDee sat with a group of friends, trying not to look forlorn. Elizabeth was even starting to get a little angry at Bill for being so blind to Jessica's manipulations.

Todd shot Elizabeth a meaningful look. "Cleopatra had nothing on your sister," he muttered under his breath.

Elizabeth frowned. It was OK for *her* to be critical of Jessica, but for some reason she bristled whenever Todd made one of his barbed comments. It was probably the only real sore spot in their relationship. The one time they'd come close to breaking up was when Elizabeth had stubbornly insisted on bailing Jessica out of a jam. Jessica had been late for a test, and Elizabeth had taken it for her. Todd had been furious. But Elizabeth couldn't bear to see her twin get into trouble—even though she knew Jessica deserved it.

Elizabeth spotted a group of kids making their way down the beach. Among them was Tom McKay. Jessica must have seen him, too, for she instantly pulled away from Bill.

"Oh, gosh," she said, "all that swimming really made me hungry. In fact, I'm positively *starved*." She directed a beseeching gaze at Bill.

Bill reacted as if on cue. "I could run up to

the Dairi Burger and get you something if you want," he volunteered eagerly.

"Would you, Bill? Are you sure you wouldn't mind?" She fluttered her long eyelashes at him.

"I—I don't mind a bit."

"I'd be eternally grateful. If I don't get a snack soon, I'll positively *faint*."

Bill scrambled to his feet. "What do you feel like having?"

"Let me see. A cheeseburger—and a double order of fries. Oh, and a chocolate milkshake. I shouldn't"—she touched one flawless cheek—"but I can never resist."

Elizabeth couldn't remember the last time she'd seen her sister with a pimple.

"Anything else?" Bill asked.

"Tell them to leave off the onions. I hate onions."

"No problem." He looked around at the others. "Anybody else want anything while I'm at it?"

Elizabeth put in a request for a root beer, but at the same time she felt vaguely guilty—as if she were somehow part of a conspiracy to take advantage of Bill.

Bill was loping off in the direction of the parking lot when Tom finally reached them, accompanied by Ken Matthews, Lila Fowler, and last—but certainly not least—Patsy Webber.

"What's cookin', good lookin'?" Tom quipped, sinking down beside Jessica and draping a bronzed, muscular arm about her shoulders. His blue eyes were the color of faded denim against the deep tan of his face.

She giggled. "Nothing much was, but it looks as if things are starting to sizzle."

Elizabeth's attention was riveted on Patsy, who was positively breathtaking in a bikini that looked as if it consisted of nothing more than three tiny scraps of material and a yard or so of string. Elizabeth had never seen anything so daring, except maybe in pictures of the French Riviera. On anyone else it might have looked sleazy, but Patsy managed to appear both elegant and alluring.

"Whew, am I *hot*!" Patsy exclaimed. She dropped her beach bag on the sand next to Elizabeth, who couldn't help noticing the exclusive label. "Anybody feel like joining me in the water?"

"Are you kidding?" Lila patted her wavy, light brown hair. "When I go swimming, it's strictly frizz city."

"I wouldn't mind cooling off," said Todd, smiling up at Patsy.

Elizabeth felt as if she'd been kicked in the stomach. She didn't doubt Todd needed cooling off. His temperature had probably shot up fifty degrees the minute he laid eyes on Patsy!

"What about you, Liz?" Todd asked her. "You feel like going in for a swim?"

Elizabeth shook her head.

"You sure?" he asked again, but it didn't sound to Elizabeth as if he were trying very hard to convince her.

"Liz is afraid of sharks," Jessica teased, glancing quickly at Patsy. The double meaning was obvious.

Lila didn't pick up on it, however. "Really? I remember the first time I saw *Jaws*. I was even afraid to go swimming in our pool afterward!"

Cara laughed. "That's because your pool is the size of the Pacific Ocean," she said, making reference to the conspicuousness of the Fowlers' wealth.

"I don't believe in sharks," Tom said, nuzzling Jessica's cheek. "Only mermaids."

"Are you implying there's something fishy about me?" Jessica twittered.

"There's only one way to find out."

Everyone laughed as Tom scooped her into his arms and carried her, kicking and squealing in protest, down toward the water.

Patsy and Todd followed suit, racing side by side. Their laughter as they hit the water could be heard all the way up the beach.

Suddenly Elizabeth felt like crying. She knew exactly how DeeDee must have felt when Bill abandoned her for Jessica.

Elizabeth had wandered up to the parking area to retrieve her book from Todd's car when she spotted a bunch of girls piling out of a dusty green van driven by frizzy-haired Olivia Davidson, a friend who worked on the school paper with her. As she drew closer, Elizabeth spotted Lois Waller and Enid Rollins, too.

Enid pushed her big, round sunglasses onto the top of her head as she greeted Elizabeth. Her green eyes narrowed to a squint as she took in her best friend's miserable expression.

"You look like you've been crying," she noted with concern. "What's the matter, Liz?"

"Oh, it's nothing." Elizabeth ducked her head. She was reluctant to confide in Enid in front of the other girls. Lois Waller made her a little uncomfortable—always trying so hard to impress people, to be in the center of things. And though Elizabeth liked Olivia very much, she just wasn't as close a friend as Enid. "I—I must have gotten some sand in my eye," Elizabeth fibbed.

"The same thing happened to me the last time I was at the beach," Olivia recalled in sympathy. "Winston Egbert was clowning around as usual and accidentally kicked sand in my face. I thought I was going to go blind!"

"Please—spare me the cracks about being blind," Lois chimed in, blinking behind the thick glasses she wore. They were always slipping down her nose, no matter how often she poked them back into place. "I can't even find my way out of the shower without my glasses!"

They all laughed, and Elizabeth felt her mood lift slightly. But it sank down to her knees again as they neared the beach and she spied Todd and Patsy splashing around in the surf, batting foam at each other.

"Isn't that Patsy Webber with Todd?" Olivia asked. "I *heard* she'd moved back into the area. Boy, has she changed!"

"You know her?" Elizabeth asked.

"When Patsy lived in Palisades, my cousin Amy lived down the street from her. Gosh, I can remember when Patsy was just a skinny kid. All bones. I never could figure out what Todd saw in her. It sure looks like she really filled out in all the right places, though. Wow, I can hardly believe it!"

Elizabeth felt her heavy heart sink all the way down into her sandals.

"Todd did say he and Patsy used to be pretty close," she recalled dispiritedly.

"Close?" Olivia echoed. "Well, I guess that's one way of putting it."

Elizabeth bit her lip to keep from crying.

Enid laid a sympathetic hand on Elizabeth's shoulder, but that only made it worse. The lump in her throat swelled until she was afraid she was going to burst into tears at any second.

"Liz, don't be upset. Todd and Patsy were together ages ago," Enid pointed out. "It's practically ancient history. *You're* the one he loves."

"Enid's right," Olivia added quickly. "It

was a long time ago. I'm sure Todd's forgotten by now that he was ever in love with her."

All eyes followed Todd and Patsy as they frolicked in the water. Patsy's playful shrieks could be heard all the way up the beach.

Elizabeth swallowed hard. "They were in love?" she repeated slowly, to make sure she hadn't misunderstood.

Olivia reddened. "Oh, what's wrong with me? I think I must have terminal foot-in-mouth disease. I'm really sorry, Liz. I didn't mean to upset you. Listen, I don't know for sure whether they were in love or not. Patsy and I weren't that close, so she never told me much."

"When did they break up?" Elizabeth asked. She realized she was only torturing herself, but she had to find out.

Olivia looked more uncomfortable than ever. She twirled one brown curl around her index finger and avoided Elizabeth's gaze.

"I don't think they ever *really* broke up," she said. "I guess they just stopped seeing each other when Patsy moved away. But that doesn't mean. . . . Well, I'm sure it's not what you think. . . ." Her voice trailed off uncertainly.

Elizabeth didn't know *what* to think anymore. If Todd hadn't really broken up with Patsy, did that mean he'd never really stopped loving her? What if they got back together again? How would she feel then? The thought was too terrible to contemplate, so she pushed it to the back of her mind.

"It doesn't matter," Elizabeth said too brightly. "It's silly of me to get so worked up over this whole thing. Like you said, it happened a long time ago. I'm sure Todd has gotten over her by now."

But even as she said it, Elizabeth didn't quite believe it was true.

Jessica lay stretched on the bed, her face a twisted mask of anguish. Bill knelt beside her with his head buried in his hands.

"Oh, Bud," she whispered. "I'm sorry, but I just couldn't face the thought of life without you. . . ."

It was Tuesday, and the cast had gathered for a noon rehearsal in the auditorium. This was Jessica's biggest scene, where Deanie tries to commit suicide by drowning herself and afterward her boyfriend, Bud, feels so guilty he can hardly live with himself. Jessica, who had obviously seen more than one episode of "General Hospital," was pulling out all the stops in her performance.

DeeDee watched from the wings as Jessica lifted a limp hand to Bill's cheek. Real tears shimmered in her eyes. Bill looked as if he were on the verge of crying himself. DeeDee felt a tightening in her chest. She told herself it was because she was being swept away by Bill's performance, but deep down she knew better. The painful truth was that she was falling in love with Bill.

It was hopeless, she told herself. Utterly hopeless. Bill liked her, but only as a friend. As far as anything more went, she might as well be invisible. At least, as long as he went on being blinded by Jessica's brilliance.

Someone jostled her elbow, and she turned to see Roger Barrett staring so fixedly at Lila Fowler he didn't even notice he'd bumped into DeeDee. Lila played Deanie's mother, and Roger had a small walk-on part. DeeDee had never paid much attention to Roger in the past—probably because he seemed so secretive and kept mostly to himself—but at the moment she felt a sudden flaring of kinship between them. It was obvious Roger had a crush on Lila, one that was even more hopeless than DeeDee's crush on Bill. Lila was definitely out of Roger's league.

Then DeeDee's attention was diverted back to what was happening onstage.

Jessica threw her arms around Bill, burying her face against his chest. "Bud, oh, Bud!" she choked.

DeeDee sighed. Bill was so good-looking, even though he didn't seem to realize it. And so natural. In her mind she saw him as he rocketed through a wave, the wind whipping the wet strands of hair back from his face, his blue eyes matching the color of the water.

As Bill took Jessica in his arms, planting a tender kiss on her lips, DeeDee's eyes filled with tears. When it was over, she was the only one who wasn't applauding.

"You sure disappeared in a hurry after rehearsal," Bill said, putting his tray down beside DeeDee's at the cafeteria table.

DeeDee looked up, surprised and pleased that he had sought her out. The tempo of her heart picked up. Maybe there was a chance. . . .

"I—I was starving," she lied. "And we don't have much time to eat on rehearsal days."

"There was something I wanted to ask you," he said, sitting down and regarding her seriously.

Her pulse was hammering so loudly in her ears that she could hardly hear herself speak. "There was?"

"Actually, I wanted your opinion. You know the scene we were doing? Do you think I overplayed it? Jessica says I—"

"You were perfect, Bill," DeeDee interrupted. "I can't imagine how you could play it better." She had a feeling Jessica just didn't like being upstaged, but she refrained from making any comment.

"You really think so?" Bill's face lit up at her praise.

"I've been telling you all week how good you are," she scolded playfully. "Haven't you been listening?"

"I guess I just have a hard time believing it." He absentmindedly munched on a pickle spear.

"It's like what *you're* always telling *me* about surfing," DeeDee said. "Half of it is just having confidence in yourself."

He grinned sheepishly. "You're right. But when I'm up on that stage, it doesn't feel the same as shooting a curl."

DeeDee laughed. "I can just see it. The audience is going wild, and instead of taking a bow, you paddle off into the wings."

They both started laughing.

"What's so funny, you two?" a silken voice intruded.

DeeDee looked up just as Jessica adroitly slid in between them and set down her tray. Instantly Bill was reduced to Jell-O.

"Uh, hi, Jessica," he mumbled. Not knowing what else to say, he forked in a mouthful of potato salad. But he swallowed too quickly and fell into a fit of coughing.

"Am I interrupting anything?" Jessica inquired sweetly.

"No—no, of course not!" Bill recovered.

DeeDee was torn between wanting to melt under the table and wanting to stab Jessica with her fork.

"We were just talking about the play," she said, trying to keep her voice even.

Jessica gave Bill the full benefit of her dimpled smile. "It really went well today, didn't it? Mr. Jaworski says we'll have to hand out handkerchiefs at the door if we get any more convincing. Oh, I get goose bumps just thinking about it! Of course, I'm just a block of wood compared to you, Bill."

"Are you kidding?" Bill was blind to Jessica's obvious attempt at soliciting compliments. He leaped to her defense like a tiger. "I could never be as good as you in a million years! You're practically good enough to be in the movies."

"Really?" Jessica preened. "You really think so?"

Bill looked past Jessica to DeeDee, oblivious to her anguish. "Don't you think she's great, DeeDee?"

Now it was DeeDee's turn to choke. Somehow, though, she managed to squeeze out a reply. "Sure," she said weakly.

But Jessica wasn't listening. It was more than apparent that she couldn't care less what DeeDee's opinion of her was. She peeled back her hamburger bun and looked dismayed.

"Oops! Would you believe I forgot the ketchup? My mind must be a million miles away!"

"I'll get it for you." Bill practically fell over in his haste to get up.

If Jessica had asked him to throw himself off a skyscraper, DeeDee thought, he'd probably ask her what floor.

"Oh, Bill, you're absolutely the *sweetest,*" Jessica gushed. "Honestly, sometimes I just don't know what I'd do without you around. . . ."

DeeDee felt sick. Her lunch sat in her stomach in a hard lump. Bill, on the other hand, was positively glowing as he rushed off to do Jessica's bidding.

"Excuse me," DeeDee mumbled, pushing away from the table and picking up her tray. She hoped she could make it outside before she burst into tears.

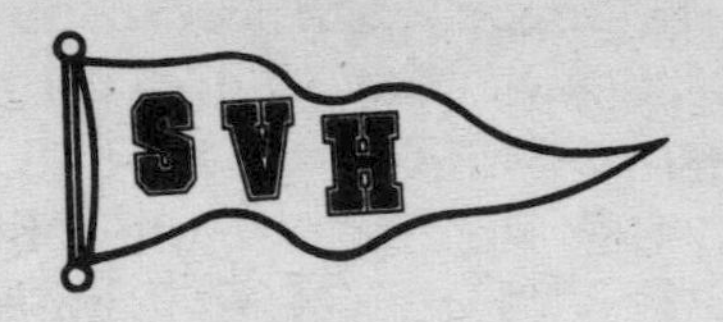

Five

"Score another one for your sister," Todd commented as he observed the scene from the next table. "I'll say this for Jessica—she sure knows how to make a monkey out of Bill."

Elizabeth shifted uncomfortably in her seat. "That's not fair. We can't hear what she said."

"Did you see the look on DeeDee's face? Talk about one picture being worth a thousand words!"

Elizabeth was silent as she pushed her food around on her plate with her fork. Her appetite hadn't been the same since the weekend, when Todd had practically thrown himself at Patsy at the beach. Elizabeth hadn't confronted him about it, but she'd made it a point to ask around the past couple of days—and what she discovered had only made her feel a million times worse.

Not only had Todd been seeing Patsy before she moved away, they'd been dating *only* each other. Now she was back—more gorgeous and sophisticated than ever, according to those who'd known her before. Elizabeth felt a stab of uneasiness every time she thought about it, which lately had been about a hundred times a day.

She longed to talk to Todd about it. They'd always been so close, no secrets between them. But this really had her worried. She was afraid of what she might find out if she asked for the truth. She tried to push this problem to the back of her mind and refocus on the one at hand.

"I know DeeDee's probably jealous, but it's not Jessica's fault she's got the lead opposite Bill," Elizabeth said. She felt compelled to defend her sister, even though she secretly believed Todd was right.

"What I saw just now didn't look like any rehearsal to me. Come off it, Liz. We've been through this before. *I* know what Jessica is like. You don't have to defend her to me."

"If you know her so well, then you must also know that she can be really sweet a lot of the time."

"Sweet like a barracuda." Todd shoved in the last bite of his hamburger.

Elizabeth leaped to her feet. "You just don't know when to quit, Todd!"

Instantly he was contrite. From the look on his face, he obviously knew he'd gone too far.

He put out a hand to stop her from running away.

"Look, Liz, I'm sorry. You're right. I shouldn't have opened my big mouth."

"You said it!"

Elizabeth knew she was probably overreacting, but keeping her feelings to herself about Patsy for so long had really put her on edge. It was like sitting on a time bomb. Nevertheless, she struggled to keep her temper.

"OK, let's forget it," she muttered. "I'll meet you after school."

"I'll be at the rehearsal," Todd said. "I promised Bill I'd stick around."

As she walked toward her locker, Elizabeth couldn't help wondering about all the time Todd had been spending at rehearsals lately. But she'd been pretty busy herself, working on an article for the school paper on summer job opportunities, so she really couldn't complain. It wasn't until she ran into DeeDee in the corridor that things started falling into place.

DeeDee seemed to have recovered from the incident in the cafeteria. Her eyes looked a little red, but any unhappiness she might have been feeling was masked by the warm smile with which she greeted Elizabeth.

DeeDee groaned laughingly as she held up the enormous shopping bag full of clothes she was lugging. "Costumes for the play," she explained. "Patsy's really been going all out collecting this stuff. Personally, I think she's gone a little overboard. I mean, this isn't exactly Broadway."

"Patsy?" Elizabeth echoed.

"Yeah, she's doing the costumes for the play. Didn't Todd or Jessica tell you?"

Elizabeth shook her head slowly. "No."

"Actually, it was Todd's idea. He told Mr. Jaworski how Patsy used to model clothes for this boutique in Paris. You've got to admit, she's really got style. I'm not sure Sweet Valley High is ready for her, though."

Elizabeth was speechless. A dull, hammering fear had started up inside her.

Suddenly it was all horribly clear—the reason Todd had been spending so much time at rehearsals, the reason he'd tried to pick a fight with her at lunch. It didn't take a genius to figure it out. Todd was interested in Patsy—as more than just a friend.

Elizabeth fought the urge to run away. While DeeDee chattered on about the play, Elizabeth bit her lip to keep from crying. The ache in her chest was getting worse and worse.

She was so wrapped up in her misery, she practically plowed into Enid, who was trudging toward her next class.

"Whoa!" Enid cried. "What's with you, Liz? You look like you just found out you flunked every course. And I *know* that can't be it."

"Oh, Enid . . ." Elizabeth let out a long, shuddery sigh. "It's Todd."

"Uh-oh, I thought so. I haven't seen you look this upset since the last time you two almost broke—" She clapped a hand over her mouth. "Oh, Liz, it's not that, is it? You and Todd haven't broken up!"

Elizabeth shook her head. "No. Not yet, anyway. It's just that I have this awful feeling. . . ."

Enid's wide green eyes took on a sudden sharp gleam. "This feeling of yours wouldn't happen to be about five feet nine with red hair and a gorgeous body, would it?"

"How did you know?"

"I'm not your best friend for nothing, remember? I knew you were upset that day at the beach, even though you tried to shrug it off."

Elizabeth sighed. "Was I that obvious?"

"Let's just put it this way. If an old girlfriend of George's suddenly popped up looking like a clone of Bo Derek, I'd be worried, too. No, I take that back. I'd be climbing the walls!"

Elizabeth managed a watery smile. "I'm glad you understand."

Enid always did. She was sensitive to other people's problems, but she was never quick to judge. It was one of the reasons Elizabeth loved her.

"Look," Enid said, taking her by the elbow

and steering her off into the corner by the drinking fountain where they could talk without being overheard. "I said I know how you feel, but that doesn't necessarily mean it's true that Todd's interested in Patsy. He really loves you, Liz. It would take a lot to change that."

"Do you really think so?"

"You're probably blowing this whole thing out of proportion."

Elizabeth stared down at her feet. "Maybe I am. I don't know."

"Has he actually said anything to you about Patsy?"

"No—not exactly." She told Enid about the play.

"Todd did say she was a friend," Enid pointed out. "And friends look out for each other, right? Sounds to me like he was just doing her a favor."

"I hope you're right." Elizabeth didn't feel very convinced, though.

"This whole thing is crazy, anyhow. You should be talking to Todd about it, not me. How's he supposed to know what's on your mind unless you tell him?"

"I guess I'm just afraid." Elizabeth grimaced. "It's sort of like when I was a kid and I'd cover my eyes when I knew a scary part was coming up in a movie. What if I ask Todd how he feels about Patsy and he tells me he wants to break up?"

"Come on, Liz. Do you really think that will happen? Just because Todd recommended her for some dumb job as a costume designer?"

Elizabeth thought for a long moment. Finally she shook her head. "I don't know, Enid. I just don't know."

"What's the matter, Bill?" Todd asked. "You look kind of down. Nervous about the play?"

Bill had been lost in thought, but he looked up as his friend dropped down beside him on the locker room bench. The rest of the class had headed out to the gym already, but Bill was in no hurry to join them.

"Sure, I'm a little nervous," he admitted, bending to tie his shoelace. "I wasn't thinking about the play, though."

Todd gave him a sympathetic look. "Jessica, right?" he said softly. "Look, I don't mean to butt in or anything—you haven't asked my advice, so I should probably keep my big mouth shut—but I hate to see you like this."

Bill reddened. "That transparent, huh?"

"Well, let's put it like this—the way you've been falling all over yourself to get her attention, you should probably take out accident insurance." Todd slung an arm around Bill's hunched shoulders. "Just don't let her take advantage of you, OK?"

"I—I like doing things for Jessica," Bill stammered.

"Not as much as *she* likes it," Todd said. "Look, I know love is blind, but don't be *too* blind."

"*You're* in love with Liz, and she's Jessica's twin," Bill defended weakly.

"Jessica's not Liz," Todd said. "They may look alike, but that's where the similarity ends. Don't make the same mistake I made in the beginning."

"What mistake?"

"For a little while Jessica had me thinking *she* was the one I should be going after when all along it was Liz I really liked."

"How did you know Liz was the one?" Bill asked shyly.

"Well, for one thing, I could really talk to Liz. We were friends. I happen to think that's pretty important. Two people really have to like each other if it's going to be a good relationship."

Bill nodded slowly. That's the way it had been with Julianne. She wasn't just his girlfriend, she was his best friend. They could just hang out together, talking about everything under the sun or feeling comfortable not talking at all. He had to admit it wasn't that way with Jessica. But did love have to be the same every time?

"Thanks for the advice, Todd," Bill said, rising stiffly. "But don't worry, I can take care of myself."

Todd looked up at him with a concerned expression. "Hey, Bill, you're not mad, are you? Maybe I shouldn't have said anything. . . ."

"No, I'm not mad at you, Todd," Bill said.

As he walked away, he realized it was the truth. He *was* angry, but not at Todd. The person he was angry with was himself. Only he didn't know why.

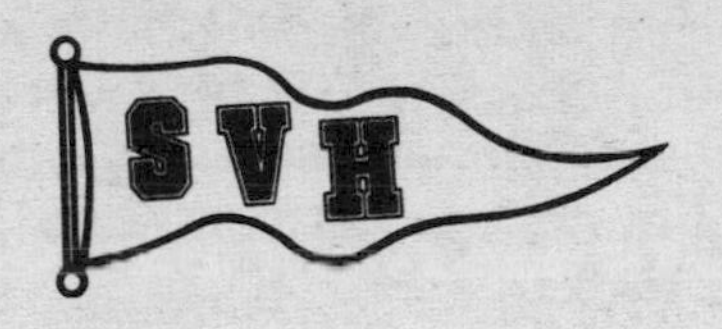

Six

Jessica wiped a damp strand of hair from her eyes. It had to be at least five hundred degrees, she thought, and they'd been stuck indoors rehearsing all morning! And she'd always thought Saturdays were for fun. She glanced at Bill, who was carrying on an animated conversation with DeeDee over by a stack of props. Well, the day wasn't over yet. . . .

Jessica sidled up to Bill, snaking an arm through his. "I'm so hot I could absolutely *die*. What do you say we all go over to my house and dive into the pool?"

Like mercury rising in a thermometer, a slow flush crept up the sides of Bill's neck until it had turned the tips of his ears bright red.

"Gee, Jessica, I'd like to"—his eyes shifted uneasily from Jessica to DeeDee—"but I promised DeeDee I'd take her surfing."

Jessica knew all about the surfing lessons.

Bill had been taking DeeDee out a lot lately. He couldn't stop bragging about how good she was becoming—something that was really starting to get on Jessica's nerves. According to Bill, DeeDee had gotten good enough to enter the Women's Junior Surfing Championship, which would be held in two weeks. With the play also two weeks away, Jessica couldn't help wondering where on earth either of them found the time or energy. She was doubly annoyed by the fact that it didn't fit in at all with the image she liked to have of Bill sitting around at home pining for her.

Artfully, she let her smile drop, as if the disappointment were too much to bear. "Oh, that's really too bad, Bill. I was counting on having you there. I wanted to make up for missing our last date." She glanced briefly at DeeDee. "Of course, you're invited, too," she added as an afterthought.

DeeDee didn't reply. She was staring at Bill with a stricken expression, waiting for him to make up his mind, waiting for him to choose between her and Jessica.

Bill hesitated only a moment before conscience won out. "Maybe next time," he mumbled.

Jessica was fuming. She couldn't believe that any boy, much less someone who was supposed to be as infatuated with her as Bill was, would rather be off with dorky old DeeDee when he could be with *her*.

She slid her hand lightly down Bill's arm, curling her fingers over his. "It's just that it won't be much fun without you. But don't worry—I understand. Why would you want to swim around in our dinky little pool when you could have the whole Pacific Ocean?"

Bill's response was to turn even redder. "It's not that, Jessica. I really would like to come. But I promised D—"

DeeDee couldn't stand it a minute longer. "That's OK, Bill," she cut in swiftly. "Why don't you go ahead? I really think I need to practice on my own for a change." She forced a cheery smile, but inside her heart was breaking.

Bill made only a very feeble attempt to talk her out of it. "Are you sure?" Relief was written all over his face.

"Sure I'm sure. If I'm going to enter the championship, it's going to look awfully funny having you holding my hand the whole time. Of course, I could always say you were my Siamese twin, but I'm not sure they'd buy it."

DeeDee knew she was running off at the mouth, making jokes to cover up for what she was really feeling. It was an old defense that dated back to when she'd been a chubby little girl and the only way she could keep the other kids from making cracks about her was to make them laugh first. DeeDee's smile was plastered on so tightly that it was beginning to ache. Tears stung behind her eyelids.

"I think DeeDee is absolutely right," Jessica put in. "A girl really needs to be self-sufficient these days."

No sooner were the three of them outside than Jessica gave a tiny cry and turned to Bill. "Oh, dear, I must have left my script back onstage. Would you mind terribly, Bill? . . ."

Of course he didn't. DeeDee couldn't stand to watch. Around Jessica, Bill was like a puppet, with you-know-who pulling the strings. Mumbling an excuse, DeeDee rushed off before Bill could return. With her chin tucked low against her chest to hide her tears, she didn't see where she was going and nearly collided with Roger Barrett.

"Aren't you going swimming over at Jessica's?" she asked, hoping to put him at ease with a little conversation. If such a thing were possible, he looked even more flustered than she felt.

"I—I didn't feel like it," he stammered, blushing.

It was obvious he was hiding the real reason for not wanting to go, but DeeDee didn't want to pry. Now that she thought about it, it seemed Roger was always rushing off as if he had something important to do but didn't want anyone to know what it was.

Maybe he was a spy, she thought. The idea would have made her laugh if she'd been in a better mood. Roger, with his shaggy haircut and scuffed loafers, and the glasses that kept slipping down his nose, was a far cry from James Bond. It wasn't that he was bad-looking. Underneath his glasses and misfit clothes, she suspected he could even be handsome. The trouble was, he lacked confidence.

DeeDee felt sorry for him. She knew what it was like being on the outside looking in. In her case, it had always been "good old DeeDee." Everybody's friend, nobody's girlfriend. Especially not Bill's, she thought. He'd made that perfectly clear, hadn't he?

"Well, see you." DeeDee waved at Roger as she headed off toward her car in the parking lot.

She knew she should get to the beach while the tide was still up, but suddenly she didn't feel like hurrying. Suddenly the beach seemed like the loneliest place in the world.

"Watch, everybody! I'm going to attempt the famous Wakefield dive!"

Bill shaded his eyes against the sun, but nothing could protect him from the dazzling sight of Jessica as she stood poised on the end of the diving board in a white bikini that showed off her golden tan. Bill's own heart executed a dive as she raised her arms and did a running jump that sent her sailing out over the clear turquoise water. She landed cleanly, barely ruffling the water's surface as she disappeared below it. The kids who were scattered around the pool broke into spontaneous applause and hoots as she emerged wearing a triumphant grin.

"Good going, Jess!" Tom McKay called.

Tom wasn't part of the drama club crowd. He'd stopped by on his way back from a tennis match over at the country club. Bill envied the easy, confident way Tom could banter with Jessica. He wished he didn't get so tied up in knots every time he spoke to her.

Suddenly Tom was in the water beside Jessica. He grabbed her by the waist while she squealed with laughter and tried to splash water in his face. Watching them, Bill felt a surge of jealousy. Jessica had acted as if she really wanted him to come in the beginning, but ever since Tom had arrived, she'd really ignored him.

The way you ignored DeeDee, a tiny voice inside reminded him.

At the thought of DeeDee, Bill immediately felt guilty. He shouldn't have dropped her like that, even though she'd insisted. She was a good friend, and he had promised he'd take her surfing. He was really proud of the progress she'd made. She was a fast learner, and a terrific sport, too. Besides, she was someone he could really talk to. With DeeDee, he could open up and be himself, the way he'd been with Julianne.

Bill winced at the memory. True, DeeDee didn't look like Julianne the way Jessica did, but there were other similarities. They shared the same easy, bubbling laugh, they were both sympathetic listeners, and they were naturals when it came to surfing.

He quickly brushed aside the comparison. How could he be thinking about DeeDee this way when Jessica was the one he cared about?

Jessica squirted a mouthful of water at Tom, and he retaliated by dunking her under. They were really having a great time, Bill thought glumly. He understood about Tom—he really did. Why should Jessica allow herself to be tied down to one guy when she could have her pick of fifty million others?

The trouble was, Bill didn't normally go in for the crowd scene and standing in line. It was one reason he spent so much time in the water. It was so quiet out there, really peaceful, with the waves lapping against his surfboard, and the cries of the sea gulls keeping him company. He'd explained it to DeeDee one time, and she had really seemed to understand.

Somehow he didn't think Jessica would

have understood. Looking at her now, as she climbed out of the pool with Tom at her heels, both of them laughing, Bill felt a surge of despair.

Being in love was a lot like getting wiped out by a wave, he thought.

Elizabeth could hear the splashing and laughter coming from the backyard as she pulled the little red Fiat Spider into the driveway. It was such a hot day that she'd put the top down even though the ride from the library was a short one. She had just spent a couple of stuffy hours researching the term paper she was working on for her civics class.

Her father greeted her as she walked inside. He was sitting on the living room couch, bent over a pile of papers spread across the coffee table. Elizabeth was struck, as she often was, by how athletic her father looked for someone who spent so much of his time at a desk poring over legal briefs. He was tall enough to be a basketball player, with the densely muscled trimness of a swimmer or track star.

"Hi," she said, flopping down on the couch beside him. "What are you doing shut up inside on such a glorious day?"

"I'm hiding out," he confessed, chuckling. "I'm not sure, but judging from the sound of it,

I think a band of Apaches has taken over the backyard."

"Jess and the drama crowd?"

"Yup." Ned Wakefield winked. "And either Jessica's been taken captive or it's the other way around. I vote for the latter."

Elizabeth rolled her eyes but couldn't suppress a giggle. "Oh, Dad, be serious!"

"I'm serious all week long in court. Don't you think I'm entitled to a few laughs on the weekend?" He gave a mock sigh of exasperation.

Alice Wakefield sailed in from the kitchen, where she had been in the midst of preparing guacamole dip.

"Your sister's got the whole gang over," she explained. Outside, there was a scream, followed by a splash. "If you ask me, it sounds like they're rehearsing the Pearl Harbor scene from *From Here to Eternity*."

"I'd better get into my suit before all the water's gone," Elizabeth said, bolting for the stairs.

"Todd's out there, too," her mother called after her.

Todd! Elizabeth's mouth went dry, and her heart beat at a quickened pace. She hadn't seen much of him these past few days—both of them had been so busy—and she'd really missed him. She felt a little silly now about the way she'd doubted him. She'd made such a big thing out of Todd's being nice to an old girlfriend.

She imagined confronting him with her fears. Todd would laugh and tell her how crazy she was for thinking he could be in love with someone else—even someone as gorgeous as Patsy. He'd take her in his arms and with one kiss blot out all the misery of this past week.

Elizabeth hurriedly slipped into her striped two-piece bathing suit and snatched a towel from the bathroom she shared with her sister. After giving her reflection a quick once-over in the mirror on her way out the door, she ended up yanking the rubber band off her ponytail. There. With her hair shimmering loose about her shoulders, she looked much more seductive. More like Jessica, she decided, a twinkle of secret amusement creeping into her eyes.

Wild shrieks and a tumult of splashing greeted her as she stepped out through the sliding glass patio door. She was momentarily blinded by the sun's glare, but then the scene before her sharpened into focus.

Elizabeth gave a muffled cry at what she saw. There was Todd, crouching over Patsy as she lay stretched in golden, queenly splendor on the chaise longue. She was on her stomach, and the back tie to her bikini top was undone.

Todd was rubbing suntan lotion on her back with slow, circular strokes.

At that moment he looked up, and his eyes met Elizabeth's. He stood up as if to greet her, but she'd already fled back inside.

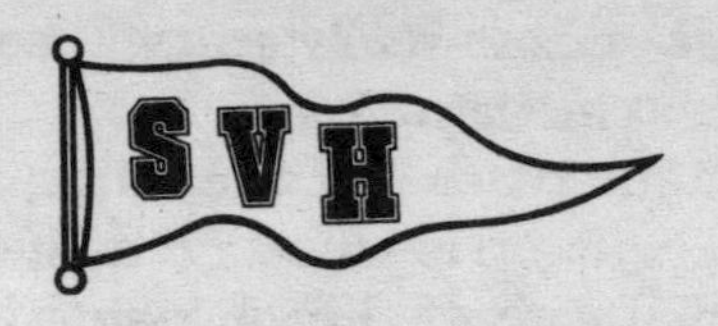

Seven

"Liz, *please,* talk to me. I want to know what the heck is going on!"

Todd's concerned voice filtered through the locked bedroom door, causing Elizabeth to spill a fresh torrent of tears. Why was he pretending to be so innocent? Did he think she was blind?

"I don't want to talk!" came her reply, muffled by the pillow she had pulled over her head. "And I'm canceling our date for tonight!"

But Todd wasn't the type to give up easily. "Liz, this is crazy. You've been acting really strange these past few days. Are you sure you're all right?"

"I'm just fine!"

"Look, if it's because I was rubbing suntan oil on Patsy's back . . ."

So he knew she wasn't blind after all! "Rub all you like. I couldn't care less!"

"Liz, this is really crazy," he repeated. "It was just a little sun—"

But Elizabeth had shut out his feeble explanations with her pillow. She couldn't bear to listen to any more. The evidence had been right there before her eyes.

Even so, she longed to believe Todd, to let herself be convinced it was all a hideous mistake. But it was useless. She might have inherited her looks from her mother, but her rock-hard sense of logic had come straight from her father. It was logical for Todd to fall in love with Patsy. And there were simply too many places in Todd's life where Patsy fit in just a little too neatly.

Gingerly she lifted the pillow from her head. The thud of receding footsteps sounded Todd's retreat. For some reason that only made her feel worse. She felt abandoned, even though *she* was the one who had told him to leave. She couldn't help thinking that if he really cared, he would have tried a little harder to convince her.

Abruptly the door to the bathroom that connected the twins' bedrooms burst open. Jessica, dripping wet, hurtled across the room to throw her arms around her sister.

"I was coming up for extra towels, and I saw Todd. He said you'd locked yourself in your room and wouldn't talk to anyone. But I *know* you couldn't have meant me! Oh, Liz, what is it? Did you two have a fight?"

Todd was wrong about Jessica, Elizabeth

thought. Her sister really did have a good heart, even if it didn't always seem that way. Still, she was quick to disengage herself from Jessica's damp embrace.

"I guess you can't call it an argument when you're not even speaking to someone," she sniffled, brushing the wetness from her cheeks.

"Todd must have done something really awful to make you feel this way. You know, I've always suspected he was kind of a rat."

Elizabeth wasn't sure she liked hearing Todd called a rat, even if she did feel like boiling him in oil at the moment.

She sighed. "I guess I really shouldn't blame Todd so much. I mean, Patsy is—is—well, *look* at her. What boy wouldn't be attracted to her?"

"Todd and Patsy?" Jessica's eyes widened. "I didn't know anything was going on between them."

"Todd used to go out with her before he met me. Before she moved away."

"How come I'm just now finding all this out? For heaven's sake, Liz, why didn't you tell me sooner?" She made it plain how hurt she was that Elizabeth hadn't confided in her.

Suddenly the tables had turned, and Elizabeth was consoling Jessica. "I'm sorry, Jess. I wanted to tell you. It's just that—well, you've been so busy with the play and all. It seems like I hardly see you anymore."

The truth was, Jessica was usually too involved in her own romantic exploits to pay much attention to Elizabeth's. But she had always resented the relationship between Todd and her sister. There were two big reasons why. Number one: In the beginning she'd wanted him for herself, and he'd passed her over for Elizabeth. Number two: He monopolized entirely too much of her sister's time.

"Hmmm." Jessica stared down at the bedspread, plucking at a loose thread. "Now that you mention it, I *have* noticed Todd spending a lot of time with Patsy at rehearsals. They must have been pretty close, huh?"

Elizabeth's heart dropped down another notch. It was one thing to have suspicions, another to have them confirmed.

"Oh, but I'm sure it doesn't mean anything," Jessica was quick to throw in. "Maybe he's just being nice because she's sort of new and stuff. He probably doesn't even want to, only he feels obligated."

"Obligated? Jess, have you really looked at Patsy? Can you imagine any guy feeling *obligated* to be nice to her?"

"I guess you're right. But honestly, Liz, there's no reason to go off the deep end about it. There are other things besides looks."

Elizabeth groaned and rolled over onto her back. "Right now I can't think of any."

"Anyway," Jessica plowed on mercilessly, "if he really is in love with her, it's probably just temporary. You know, like a crush. I'm sure it'll pass."

"Jess!" Elizabeth sat bolt upright. "Do you really think he's in love with her?"

Jessica lifted her shoulders in an exaggerated shrug. "How would I know? But if you ask me, it does look kind of suspicious."

Elizabeth moaned and buried her face in her pillow once again. How was it that whenever Jessica tried to console her, she always ended up feeling worse?

Writing was one of the few things that made Elizabeth feel better when she was really down. It had always been that way, since the day she'd started filling the pages of her very first diary, when she was nine or ten. Now she not only kept a journal faithfully but also worked as a reporter and columnist for *The Oracle*, the school paper. At the moment her article on summer job opportunities was coming along nicely.

After crying her eyes out over Todd for nearly an hour, Elizabeth decided to spend the rest of the afternoon working on the article as an antidote to her misery. It was a poor substitute for Todd, but it was certainly better than sitting around feeling sorry for herself.

Her father had promised to get her an interview with the man who owned the building his office was in. Mr. Pendergast often hired teenagers, though it was rumored he only did so to save money. Elizabeth knew he worked on Saturdays, so on impulse she decided to drive over there. If he wasn't too busy, maybe he wouldn't mind talking to her for a few minutes.

Fortunately, her dad didn't mind letting her use the Fiat, since it was for a good cause. His office was a four-story gray building just off Calico Drive, only ten minutes away. Elizabeth parked the little red convertible in front, then made her way through the heavy plate-glass door. The first thing she noticed was the sharp, damp smell of disinfectant.

A boy dressed in dark green overalls was swabbing the floor with a wet mop. A janitor's pushcart full of cleaning supplies was angled alongside him. As Elizabeth walked in, the boy looked up at her in surprise. She was equally surprised. It was Roger Barrett!

"L-Liz," he stammered. "W-w-what are you doing here?"

She grinned. "I should be asking you the same thing. How come you never mentioned you worked in my dad's building? You're the one I should be interviewing for my article."

"No! Please, I—I don't want anyone to—" He stopped, his gaze dropping down to the scuffed toes of his shoes.

Roger's reaction took Elizabeth by surprise. Had she said something wrong? He almost seemed afraid of her. Then she looked at his flaming cheeks, and she knew what it was. He was embarrassed to be working as a janitor.

"I think it's great," she said softly. "I'll bet there are at least fifty kids who would love to trade places with you. There aren't really all that many good jobs for kids our age in Sweet Valley."

Roger shook his head. "I doubt it. I'll bet most of them wouldn't be caught dead doing what I do."

"I don't see what's wrong with it."

"Please, Liz, just don't tell anyone you saw me," he begged. "I—I have my reasons. Besides, they'd only make fun of me if they knew."

"I think you're wrong," Elizabeth said. "I really admire you for what you're doing. Not everyone has enough ambition to get a job on top of their schoolwork and everything else."

"Ambition?" he said in surprise. His gray eyes, magnified by his glasses, appeared startled. "I *have* to work. If I didn't, my family wouldn't be able to pay the rent!" It was apparent he hadn't meant to blurt his secret; the words had just slipped out. He hung his head in shame.

Elizabeth touched his arm. "I'm sorry, Roger, I didn't know. Of course I won't say anything. I still don't think you have anything to be embarrassed about, though. In fact, you should be proud of yourself. I'm sure your family is."

Roger offered her a weak smile. "Thanks,

Liz. I really appreciate it. I always figured you were the type who would understand."

Elizabeth felt so sorry for Roger, she temporarily forgot her own misery. Roger really wasn't someone she knew well—they shared only one class, chemistry—but she felt as if she were seeing a side of him no one else knew. She would never forget the shamed, fearful look in his eyes.

Obviously she wasn't the only one with a problem.

Eight

Jessica fluttered about backstage like someone who'd just been asked to give a command performance at the White House.

"I'm so nervous, I could just die!" she hissed to Lila. "Why didn't anyone ever tell me DeeDee's father was a Hollywood agent?"

Lila rolled her eyes. "Who would have believed it?" Everyone knew who *Lila's* father was, so she never had that problem. George Fowler was one of the richest men in Sweet Valley.

"You're right, she's not exactly the Hollywood type, is she?" Jessica clapped a hand over her mouth to stifle her giggle.

"Shhh, she'll hear you." Lila shot a warning glance over to where DeeDee was standing, talking with her father, who had decided to drop in on a special lunchtime rehearsal. The entire cast had been given special permission to cut the class just before lunch since there was a special teachers' meeting in the auditorium after school that day. "Anyway, I don't see what you're so nervous about. It's only a rehearsal."

"Easy for you to say. You're not playing the lead."

"Do you have to rub it in?" Lila stuck her nose in the air and patted the cloud of silky brown hair that swirled about her shoulders. With a perfectly straight face, she added, "Actually, if you want to know the truth, they offered me the lead role in *Raiders of the Lost Ark* before Karen Allen—but I had to turn it down."

"Harrison Ford was too much for you, right?" Jessica played along.

"No, of course not." She wrinkled her pert nose. "Harry and I got along fine. It's just that I hate snakes."

Jessica recalled the scene in the movie in which the hero and heroine were dropped into an Egyptian tomb full of snakes. Ugh! Had they really used live snakes? Maybe there was more to being an actress than she'd considered. Still, it would be fun. Jessica smiled as a new thought occurred to her. If she were a star, she would have the perfect double—Elizabeth. They could use her sister for the stunts, and it would leave her free for the juicy stuff, like kissing Harrison. She closed her eyes, imagining what it would be like. . . .

"Hey!" Lila nudged Jessica. "I was only

kidding, you know. I think you're really getting serious about all this star business."

"Why not?" Jessica demanded. "Even Jessica Lange had to start somewhere."

"Yeah," Lila twittered, "and you know where *that* was. King Kong's hairy hand. I can just see it now—*King Kong II,* starring Jessica Wakefield." She smacked her palms together. "Oops, splat!"

Both girls collapsed in giggles. They were rescued from complete hysteria by the intervention of Mr. Jaworski, announcing that it was curtain time.

Immediately Jessica was transformed into the tragic heroine once again. She wafted onstage to join hands with Bill, whom she gazed up at with an adoring expression, as if he'd just switched faces with Harrison Ford.

"Oh, Bud, don't let them keep us apart. . . ."

DeeDee was bursting with the good news when she returned from walking her father back to his car.

"Guess what, everybody? My father loved it! He said it was practically professional. But the best part is"—she took a deep breath, a smile tugging at the corners of her mouth—"he saw someone he thinks is really talented. I mean *really* talented, like maybe this person could be in the movies!"

"Who?" Jessica practically shrieked.

"He wouldn't say. He was very mysterious about it. He's afraid it would make the person too nervous."

"How can he keep us in suspense like this?" Jessica cried. "It's—it's cruel and inhuman!"

"It's just until the end of the week," DeeDee hastened to explain. "He's bringing this producer friend of his to see the play on opening night. And get this—it's the same guy who discovered Matt Dillon! He's known for finding new talent."

Jessica was jumping up and down as if a fire had been lit under her. "Ooooh, I can't stand it! Didn't he give you a hint? Just one little hint?"

"You mean something like, she has blond hair and blue eyes, and she could be the next Jessica Lange?" Lila broke in, giving her friend an amused grin.

"Oh, stop it!" Jessica wailed. "Of *course* I don't think it's me. Why on earth would he pick me? I'm the worst one in the whole play!"

As usual, Bill rushed to her defense. "The best, you mean. I can't think of anyone else it could be."

"Thanks, Bill," she demurred. "But I'm positive you're wrong."

"Well, we won't know anything until Saturday night," DeeDee said quickly. "You don't know my dad when it comes to keeping a secret.

Nobody could get it out of him. I can hardly wait to find out who it is!"

In her excitement DeeDee threw her arms around Bill. Bill looked embarrassed, but not half as embarrassed as DeeDee was when she realized what she'd done. She took a hasty step backward, nearly falling over a stack of scenery that was propped up behind her. Acting on reflex, Bill reached out to steady her. His touch was like a delicious shock; her skin tingled with awareness. She only hoped Bill wouldn't notice that she was blushing.

Jessica had noticed, though, and for the first time found that she didn't care. What did Bill have compared to the stardom that awaited her? Naturally, she wouldn't have dreamed of saying so aloud, but it was obvious which one of them DeeDee's father had earmarked for fame and fortune.

"Maybe it's Roger," Lila snickered when she and Jessica were alone in the restroom. "Now that I think of it, he does bear a striking resemblance to Robert Redford, don't you agree?"

"Who do you really think it is?" Jessica asked. She was brushing her hair, and it flew up around her head in crackling splendor.

Lila gave her a long look. "As if you didn't know already."

Jessica wore an innocent expression. "Who, me? What makes you think *I* own a crystal ball?"

"Well, I'll say one thing. You should get the Academy Award for best performance at pretending to be modest."

That did it. Jessica burst into peals of silvery laughter. "Don't worry, Lila, I won't forget you when I'm a star. You can visit my mansion in Beverly Hills, and I'll even send you a card every Christmas."

"Thanks a lot. What I want to know is who they'll pick as your leading man in your first picture. Hey, wouldn't it be great if you got Matt Dillon? He's really sexy."

"Too immature," Jessica said and sniffed. "I was thinking more along the lines of Sylvester Stallone."

"Neat." Lila giggled. "I can just see you slugging it out with him in *Rocky Five*."

"Watch it," Jessica warned, snatching up a hair spray can and aiming it at Lila. "You may be the next one on my hit list."

"Oh, I can't stand it!" Lila gasped. "Jess, you really are too much!"

Jessica smiled to herself. It wasn't the first time she'd been accused of it. And she hoped it wouldn't be the last.

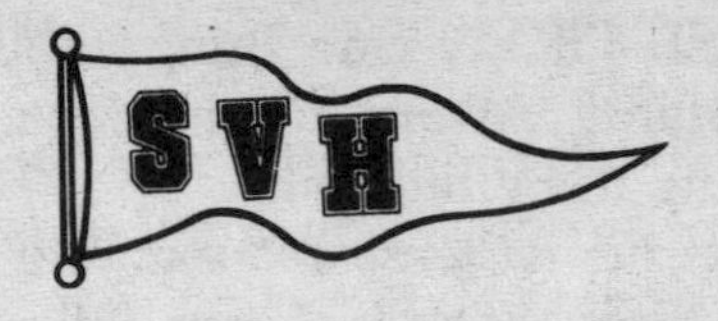

Nine

"I guess you must meet a lot of Hollywood big shots since your dad's in the business," Bill remarked.

He and DeeDee were standing outside the drama room. Most of the other cast members had already rushed off to have a quick lunch.

"Not really," DeeDee said. "You see, he doesn't live with us. My parents are divorced. We visit when we can, but he lives in L.A., so it's kind of hard to get together."

"Yeah, I know. My dad moved to Idaho after he and my mom split up. We used to be real close, and now I hardly ever see him."

"That's rough," she commiserated.

He shrugged. "Yeah, but he's really happy. He's totally switched careers. He used to be in business, and he's a forest ranger now."

"It's funny, isn't it? How people change

when they get older? I wonder what we'll be doing ten years from now?"

Bill looked thoughtful for a moment. "You know something, it's weird, but lately I've really been excited about acting. I'm actually starting to enjoy it. But if someone had told me I'd be feeling this way six months ago, I wouldn't have believed it."

DeeDee responded by giving Bill a shy smile. He'd always been pretty quiet about himself, but he was finally opening up to her.

She remembered once when she was walking in the woods and had come upon a deer grazing in a clearing. She hadn't wanted to move or even breathe too deeply for fear of scaring it off. That was how she felt now. Something had changed between them, but she didn't know what.

Bill was looking at her as if he were seeing her for the first time. Suddenly a faraway expression crossed his face, and he seemed to draw back into himself. "Hey, how's the surfing going? I'm sorry I haven't been able to go out with you these past few days, but I've been pretty tied up with this play."

DeeDee took a deep breath. "I was hoping you could go out with me today," she blurted. "Just for an hour or so. The championship is this Saturday and—I'm pretty nervous, if you want to know the truth."

"I'd like to," Bill said. "But the thing is, Jessica and I are supposed to go over these couple of scenes we're having trouble with."

At that moment Jessica breezed past them. She'd changed out of her costume into a pale blue sundress and had put on fresh lipstick that carried a faint perfumey smell. She was, as usual, breathtaking.

"Oh, Bill," she stopped to say, looking past him in a distracted way, "I forgot to tell you. I won't be able to meet you after school. Something came up. Sorry." She apologized offhandedly, as if she'd just bumped into him or stepped on his toe.

"Sure. I understand," he replied.

"I knew you would." Jessica flashed him a brief smile and was gone.

Wearing a crestfallen expression, Bill stared after her for a moment before turning back to DeeDee.

"Guess I'll have time to do a little surfing after all. That is," he faltered, "if you, uh, still want me to go with you."

She smiled. "Do I! Just meet me out at the beach at around four. OK?"

His grin was a bit wobbly, but nevertheless intact. "OK. See you then."

Elizabeth spotted her sister flying toward her across the cafeteria. Jessica's hair splashed about her shoulders in golden disarray; her cheeks were bright with color. She swooped down on Elizabeth, nearly knocking over a glass of milk as she hugged her.

"Guess what?" Jessica said. "I've got the most fantastic news in the world! DeeDee's father is going to make me a star!"

"What?" Elizabeth momentarily forgot her misery. "Is that what he said to you?"

"Not exactly. He came to our rehearsal, and afterward he told DeeDee that he thought one of us had real talent. Only he's not saying who, because he doesn't want to make anyone nervous. Isn't that just too exciting?"

"In other words," Elizabeth translated soberly, "you don't know who it is yet. It could be anybody."

Jessica's lower lip edged out in a tiny pout. "Why do you always have to be such a party pooper? Just because Todd's ignoring you, it doesn't mean you have to take your bad mood out on *me*."

Elizabeth wanted to protest that Todd hadn't been ignoring her. Just the opposite, in fact. He'd been trying to pin her down for the past few days, but she kept on avoiding him. Enid told her she was being silly and childish about the whole thing, but Elizabeth wasn't so sure.

"I'm sorry, Jess," she said wearily. "But I

just don't think it's a good idea to count on things before you know for sure."

"But it's obvious, isn't it? Who else could he have meant? I'm the best one. Everybody thinks so."

"Look, I'm not saying you're not the best. I'm just saying it's dangerous to count on something too much, that's all. Remember when you told everyone you were going to get Bruce Patman to take you to the Sophomore Fling, and he ended up asking Lila?"

Jessica's eyes narrowed to slits. "That was ages ago. I wouldn't go across the street to meet Bruce if he asked me now."

Jessica had been wild about Bruce at one time, but the experience of actually dating him had taught her what a phony he really was.

"That's not the point. I just don't want you to get your hopes up, that's all." Elizabeth sighed. "Just in case there's a chance in a billion you're wrong."

"Thanks for the advice," Jessica tossed back, "but next time I want some, I'll write to Ann Landers."

"While you're at it," Elizabeth added ruefully, "ask her what to do when your boyfriend dumps you for another girl."

But Jessica was no longer interested in Elizabeth's plight. Her head was too filled with sugarcoated visions of her own brilliant success.

She dashed off without even bothering to say goodbye.

Just then Enid came by. "Where's Jessica off to in such a hurry? New boyfriend?"

"Uh-uh. Hollywood. At least that's where she thinks she's headed. I'm not so sure." She repeated what Jessica had told her.

"It sounds pretty unbelievable to me," Enid agreed. "Then again, I've never known your sister to let anything stand in the way of getting what she wants. But what about you?" she asked, her voice softening with concern. "Have you talked to Todd?"

Elizabeth stared down at her plate. "Not yet."

"This is getting truly ridiculous. You've got to talk to him."

Elizabeth groaned. "I can't. Don't you see? I just can't. Oh, Enid, it would just be too humiliating to have him tell me what I already know."

"Aren't you forgetting one thing?"

"What?"

"That you might be wrong?"

"You didn't see them together," Elizabeth maintained stubbornly.

"Doing what? Sounds like all he was doing was rubbing suntan lotion on her back. What's the big deal?"

"It was the *way* he was doing it."

"Maybe you imagined that part."

"Am I imagining the fact that Patsy is gorgeous and sophisticated and that he used to be in love with her before he met me?"

"He *used* to be in love with her," Enid emphasized. "It doesn't necessarily mean he is now."

"But Jessica said—"

Enid frowned. "What did she say?"

"She said they spend an awful lot of time together at rehearsals."

"I'm surprised she noticed. From what I hear, Jessica spends all her time baiting poor Bill."

Elizabeth seized the opportunity to turn the subject away from her and Todd. "I think Bill may have competition before long," she said.

"Who?"

"It's my guess it's a toss-up between Richard Gere and Sylvester Stallone."

Enid giggled. "Knowing Jessica, she'll want them both. I'll bet she's got her heart set on winning an Oscar, too."

"I just hope she isn't disappointed."

"Me, too." Enid knew what Jessica was like in one of her royal rages; anyone who came within firing range was target for her anger. "For all our sakes."

* * *

Enid is right, Elizabeth said to herself as she stood at her locker after her last class.

She owed Todd a chance to explain. She couldn't go on avoiding him forever. She had to know the truth—even if the truth was that he was in love with Patsy. Determinedly she walked down the crowded hallway to Todd's locker.

She wasn't prepared for the scene that met her eyes. But this time there was no mistaking what was going on.

Todd had his arms around Patsy, and she was clinging to him in a way that left no room for doubt in Elizabeth's mind about their feelings for one another.

Hot tears flooded her eyes and scalded her cheeks. Her insides were churning. She felt as if she was going to be sick.

They didn't see her. Todd was stroking Patsy's back and murmuring something in her ear.

He's probably telling her he loves her—the way he used to tell me.

Elizabeth couldn't stand it any longer. It was like a nightmare coming true. She had to get away. She had to escape before they saw her. But she couldn't move. It was as if the air had turned to ice, freezing her body inside it.

Then, in a sudden flash of hot anguish, Elizabeth found herself pushing through the kids who were standing at their lockers or hanging around in small groups, talking. She wanted to put as much distance between herself and Todd as possible.

At that moment a million miles wouldn't have been far enough.

Ten

"Can I talk to you for a second, Jessica?" Bill caught up with her at her locker after the last bell.

"What is it?" she asked with an edge of impatience.

Swallowing the last remnants of his battered pride, Bill forced himself to speak. "I know you're busy and all, but, uh, I was wondering—" He gulped against the sudden tightness that was squeezing his throat.

"Yes?" Jessica tapped her fingernails impatiently against her locker door. "Listen, Bill, I don't mean to be rude or anything, but I'm in a big hurry. What is it you wanted to ask me?"

Bill managed to get the words out despite his humiliation. After all, this might be his last chance to win Jessica over.

"I was wondering if you might want to go to the cast party with me on opening night."

He stared down at his feet. Talking to Julianne had never been this hard. Why did he always get so tongue-tied around Jessica? "I thought—well, since we're the leads and all, it might be the thing to do."

"Sorry, Bill," Jessica said, "but I already have a date for the party. Tom's taking me."

"Oh." Bill hung his head in disappointment. "Well, I just thought I'd ask. I guess I should've known you'd be busy."

Jessica flashed him an insincere grin. "I *am* pretty busy, but don't worry. I'm sure you won't have trouble getting another date for the party. Why don't you ask DeeDee?"

"DeeDee?" Bill looked down at the floor.

"Sure. I'll bet she'd go with you in a minute."

Blushing even more furiously, Bill muttered, "I'll think about it."

Jessica scooped up her purse and books. "I'm late. Got to run."

Bill watched forlornly as she darted down the hall toward Tom McKay, who was leaning against the wall and grinning at Jessica.

Bill felt as if he'd been kicked in the stomach. Any last tiny hope he might have nourished that Jessica would ever go out with him was permanently dashed. Obviously she couldn't care less about him. It was hopeless, completely hopeless. She'd even encouraged him to take DeeDee instead.

Well, maybe he would. Maybe he'd show Jessica. And maybe he'd even enjoy taking DeeDee. At least with DeeDee he didn't have to feel awkward and foolish. He could relax and not worry about whether the things he said sounded dumb. His flattened spirits rose slightly when he realized he was looking forward to surfing with her this afternoon. Even if he was doomed to be unlucky in love for the rest of his life, it was nice to know there was at least one girl he liked who liked him back.

"Paddle faster!" Bill yelled above the pounding surf. "You've got to pick up speed so you're in the right position to shoot into the curl. Here, let me show you."

He angled his board as he paddled furiously into the next wave. DeeDee watched in admiration as he glided down the green slope of the swell with seemingly effortless grace. The wind tore the top off the wave, flinging speckles of foam back at her. That day the swells were larger than she'd ever seen them—almost scary. DeeDee fought hard to keep her balance as the choppy sea rolled beneath her board. The water seemed colder, too. Even in her wet suit she was shivering.

Nevertheless, nothing could have induced her to trade the challenge of the ocean and these precious moments alone with Bill for the safety and comfort of shore. DeeDee was never happier than when she and Bill were surfing together. The waves were Bill's domain, and he had invited her to be a part of it. Not even Jessica would dare come between them out here on a rough day like this.

But DeeDee knew Bill was thinking about Jessica, and she couldn't do anything about that. At least he was trying hard not to let his misery show. She would have to be satisfied with that, and learn to accept the fact that Bill would never see her as anything more than a friend.

But the truth was that it hurt, no matter how hard she tried to convince herself it didn't. DeeDee longed to have Bill look at her the way he looked at Jessica. But that was hopeless, wasn't it? She would never be even half as beautiful or popular as Jessica. Not in a million years.

The wave had leveled into swirls of foam. Bill touched down, then turned to wave at DeeDee with two fingers held high in the victory sign. DeeDee's chest felt tight. It was no use denying she was in love with Bill. The trouble was, he would always be too blinded by Jessica to see it.

"Your turn!" Bill shouted out to her over the churning, gray-green expanse.

A new set of swells was rolling in. They were enormous. DeeDee was scared, but she didn't want to let Bill down. He was counting on her to do her best. If she acted like a baby now, what chance did she have of placing in the championship?

Ignoring the knot of fear in her stomach, she dropped down flat on the board, propelling herself forward with a flurry of frantic strokes. Then, suddenly, she was no longer moving under her own momentum. The swell picked her up, flinging her forward. DeeDee lifted herself quickly into a low crouching position as Bill had taught her to do. She flexed her trembling knees, fighting to hold her balance as the board shook and swayed underneath her.

The wave was much bigger and more powerful than any she'd ever ridden before. She was having trouble staying on her feet. She blinked. The icy spray stung her face like handfuls of sand. Bill was a distant, blurry speck. The shore seemed a thousand miles away.

The board tilted up at the nose. Foam was boiling wildly all around her. *Your timing is off!* she could hear Bill saying inside her head. She entered the wave a second too late. It was breaking over her instead of underneath her.

DeeDee fought desperately to stay on, to keep from flying out of control. She opened her mouth to shout to Bill, but the sound was lost in the surging thunder. The board shot out from under her and flipped over in the air. She tumbled backward, catching a glimpse of gray sky tilted at a crazy angle before she went under.

Then she was thrashing and spinning helplessly in the churning surf. Panic closed over her in a tight, wet fist. She couldn't breathe. Sand was being ground into her mouth and eyes. Something hard struck her in the temple, and a brief buzzing filled her head before everything went totally black.

Bill was so lost in his misery over Jessica, it was several crucial seconds before he noticed that DeeDee had vanished from sight. His first thought was that the wave had washed her in farther down the beach. Then he saw her board. It bounced over the waves and skimmed to a stop on the sand. Bill stood frozen as he scanned the horizon.

OK, he told himself. She *had* to be OK. At the same time, he knew how easy it was for even a good swimmer to be sucked into an undertow and lose control. A friend of his had once been knocked unconscious by his board and had nearly drowned. Bill was gripped with guilt. He should never have taken her out on a day like this. The surf was just too unpredictable. She wasn't experienced enough to handle it. If anything happened to DeeDee . . .

He caught a glimpse of her, and he gave a sigh of relief. It was a second or two before he realized that she wasn't swimming, that she was facedown in the water.

Instantly Bill was galvanized into action. Every other thought except that of rescuing DeeDee was blotted from his mind as he dove into the crashing surf. He had to save her. He couldn't let her drown. Suddenly the idea of losing her was too unbearable to imagine.

Bill was a strong swimmer. Less than a minute more had passed by the time he reached her. She was unconscious. He might already be too late, he realized sickly. She didn't resist as he slipped an arm about her rib cage, supporting her against his chest the way he'd been taught in the lifesaving course he'd taken the previous summer.

"Don't worry, DeeDee," he gasped, "you're going to be OK. . . .You're going to make it. . . ."

She wasn't responding. Terror washed over him. He couldn't even tell if she was breathing. Her face was a frightening blue-white color. The bruise on her temple where her board had struck her stood out like a smear of red paint on a white canvas.

Bill swam harder than he ever had in his life. It was almost as if there were someone outside him, guiding his arms and legs, giving him a strength he didn't know he had.

He swam blindly, struggling to keep DeeDee's head above water. His eyes were stinging so badly he could scarcely see. He wasn't sure if it was the salt from the water or from his tears.

Then he had her stretched out on the wet sand. He pressed down hard against her stomach with the heel of his hand to push out the water she'd taken in. The bruise on her temple was darkening to an ugly purple.

Please be OK, DeeDee, please, please, please. . . .

As if in answer to his prayers, DeeDee stirred weakly and coughed. Bill felt his hopes surge. As he bent close to administer mouth-to-mouth resuscitation, he became aware of how pale her skin was next to the dark, wet swirls of her hair. How come he'd never noticed before how pretty she was? Even the freckles that stood out sharply on the bridge of her adorable snub nose seemed precious to him.

Unlike the rest of her, DeeDee's lips were warm. Warm and soft. He felt them move gently against his mouth as he lowered it to hers.

He knew now that DeeDee was very special to him. The feeling must have been there all along, tugging at him like an undertow beneath the calm surface of their friendship.

DeeDee's eyes fluttered open. Brown. They were a beautiful buttery-toffee brown. How come he'd never noticed that before, either? As Bill stared into her eyes, he suddenly felt as if *he* were the one who was drowning.

Eleven

A set of blurred features swam in front of her for a moment before she focused on a pair of concerned blue eyes and a mouth that hovered inches from her own.

"Bill . . ." DeeDee murmured weakly.

She was stopped from saying any more by the warm, gentle pressure of Bill's lips against hers. DeeDee forgot that she was half drowned and shivering with cold. She forgot that her head was throbbing as if she'd charged straight into a brick wall. The only thing she was aware of was the wet, salty warmth of Bill's kiss.

Heat flooded through her. Her frozen toes and fingers tingled as they thawed. She sighed—a long, shuddery sigh—as Bill gathered her to him in a sandy embrace. With her cheek pressed to his strong chest, she could hear the steady hammering of his heart. A strange, floaty feeling crept over her. None of what was happening seemed real somehow. Was she dreaming it?

His lips were moving over her hair, gently brushing against her cheek. His mouth closed over hers once again. At that moment they were caught in a sudden surge of white water. It swirled around them, sending up fans of foamy spray. DeeDee forgot how threatening the sea had seemed such a short while ago. Now the water felt teasing and delicious as it fizzed over her body, mingling with the salty taste of Bill's kiss.

Before they could be swept out to sea, Bill scooped DeeDee up in his arms and carried her up the beach to their towels. There he helped her strip off her wet suit, then tenderly dried her. DeeDee felt weak. When she tried to stand up, her knees collapsed beneath her, and she plopped back down on the sand.

"Hey, take it easy," Bill cautioned, sliding a a protective arm about her. "I figured I'd lost you back there. I wouldn't want to have you flaking out on me now."

"You're shaking, too," she said, content to curl up against the warm, solid bulk of his chest.

"You really had me scared," he admitted. "Boy, when you wipe out, you really know how to do it Hollywood style." He smoothed her hair away from her cheek. Gingerly he touched her bruised temple. "Are you OK now?"

"I think so. I don't even remember how it happened. It seemed like one minute I was hanging on for dear life, and the next minute you were. . . ." Her voice trailed off uncertainly.

Bill reddened. "Look, DeeDee, I know what a jerk you must think I am. I mean, there you are practically drowned, and I—I—" He hung his head. "I guess I don't know what got into me."

"Whatever it was, I'm glad it did." She laughed shakily. "You know, when we were learning mouth-to-mouth on that dumb doll in health ed, I never knew it could be so much fun."

A slow grin spread across his face. "Yeah, I know what you mean."

"Bill?"

"Yeah?"

"What I really want to say is thanks. For rescuing me. I feel like such an idiot, putting you through all that."

Bill was staring at her in an odd, intense way. "I'm the one who's been an idiot, DeeDee," he said softly. "I guess I was so flipped about Jessica, I couldn't see past the end of my nose."

"I understand, Bill. I really do."

"I mean, who was I kidding?" he went on. "As far as she was concerned, I didn't even exist—unless she wanted something."

So he hadn't been so blind to Jessica's manipulations after all, DeeDee realized. "Bill, you don't have to explain anything to me," she said.

"I want to." He cupped her face in his hands as tenderly as if she'd been a fragile, priceless treasure. "DeeDee, I must have been totally out of it not to see what a terrific person you are."

DeeDee tried to speak, but she couldn't find her voice.

"Not just terrific," he went on, "but terrific-looking, too. And a great kisser."

"Oh, Bill . . ."

He drew her closer, kissing her with a passionate tenderness that made her feel as if the sky had shaken loose and the ground had been snatched out from under her. She started to feel dizzy again. There was a strange humming in her ears.

"I love you, Bill," she whispered, only half aware that it was she, and not someone else, who had said the words.

He paused for the space of a heartbeat, then said, "I think I'm in love with you, too. In fact, I must've been all along, only I was too stupid to see it."

"What about Jessica?" she asked timidly, afraid to rock this precious boat but knowing she couldn't bear to be held in suspense.

Bill's answer left no room for doubt. "Jessica who?" he murmured as he eased her back onto the sand and covered her mouth with his.

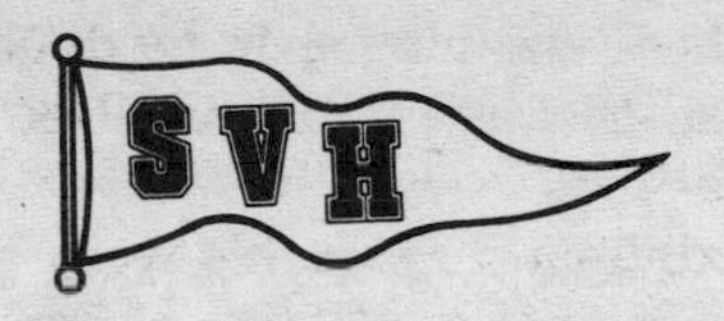

Twelve

"If you don't watch what you're doing, you're going to burn a hole in my head with that thing!" Jessica warned her sister.

Elizabeth was so wrapped up in her thoughts about Todd, she'd accidentally pressed the curling iron up against Jessica's scalp as she styled her sister's hair for the play.

"Sorry, Jess. Guess my mind was somewhere else."

Jessica let out a long, exasperated sigh. "Give me three guesses—Todd, right? You've been moping around all week about that creep. Honestly, Liz. Here I am starring in a play that could be the beginning of a Hollywood career. *I'm* the one who should be a wreck."

Clearly, she was anything but. In fact, Elizabeth thought, if her sister had been any more buoyant this past week, they would've had to anchor her to keep her from floating off into space. There was obviously no doubt in Jessica's mind that *she* was the one DeeDee's father had noticed.

By contrast, Elizabeth's week had been the longest, most miserable one of her life. She had been sick most of the week, which had enabled her to avoid Todd. But staying at home hadn't helped. Without Todd, she felt empty and alone. She tried hating him, but it was no use. The truth was she really missed him. The night before, Enid had talked her into going to a movie, but Elizabeth hadn't been able to concentrate on what was happening on the screen. All she could see was Todd and Patsy, their arms locked about one another in a passionate embrace. . . .

"Really, Liz, what did you expect?" Jessica babbled on. "I told you in the very beginning he was trouble. Something like this was bound to happen sooner or later."

Elizabeth resisted the impulse to remind her sister that she had gone after Todd herself before he made it clear he was interested in Elizabeth. Jessica was wound up as it was over this play. It wouldn't do to get her any more excited.

"I'm not mad at Todd anymore," Elizabeth replied glumly. "After all, he was in love with Patsy *before* he met me."

"There you go, making excuses again.

Honestly, Liz, there is such a thing as being *too* forgiving."

"I never heard you complain when it was *you* I was forgiving," she said, twisting a lock of Jessica's hair around the curling iron.

"Ouch! Careful, will you? I'm not starring in *The Bride of Frankenstein,* remember? I won't make much of an impression on DeeDee's father with my hair in shreds."

"Sorry."

"Look, Liz, I *am* sorry about what happened with Todd, but don't let it get you down. Anyway, he's nothing compared to the men you'll be meeting in Hollywood."

"Hollywood?" Elizabeth echoed. "What on earth are you talking about?"

"You didn't think I was going to leave you behind, did you? Lizzie, you're my very own dearest twin sister! I'd simply die if you weren't there with me."

Uh-oh, Elizabeth said silently, *here we go again.* "What exactly did you picture me doing while you're busy being a star?"

"You'll be my stand-in, of course!"

"Gee, thanks a lot, Jess."

But Jessica had obviously missed the sarcasm in her sister's voice. "Don't you see? It's absolutely perfect. What other superstar has an identical double?"

Elizabeth giggled. "If Richard Gere has one, I'd like to know where he lives."

"You could even sign autographs for me when my hand got tired. No one would have to know it wasn't me." She grinned mischievously. "And just think of all the fun we could have playing tricks on everybody."

"Sounds terrific. Too bad I won't be there to enjoy any of it."

"Why not?" Jessica looked positively offended.

"Well, actually, I'd sort of decided to throw my life away on something frivolous—like college."

"Can't you stop thinking about serious stuff for once? What's college compared to a fantastic opportunity like this?"

"Jess, you're acting as if the whole thing is already decided. Nothing's settled yet, remember?"

Jessica scowled at her. "How could I forget with my big sister constantly reminding me? Don't you have any faith in me?"

"I'm not putting you down, Jess. Honestly I'm not. I've seen you act, and I happen to think you're fantastic—onstage *and* off," she added, smiling.

"Very funny. But I'm telling you—this is a sure thing. I can *feel* it."

"I hope you're right, I really do. I just happen to be a firm believer in seeing things with my own eyes. Journalistic instinct, I guess."

"OK," Jessica said sulkily, "but if you ever

decide to become Barbara Walters the Second, don't count on me to give you an interview. I may be too busy."

Mr. Jaworski, his plump cheeks pink with excitement, stuck his head behind the backstage curtain. "I've never seen anything like it! Every seat in the auditorium is sold—now they're buying standing room!"

"I guess word has gotten out," Jessica said. "They all know DeeDee's father and his producer friend are coming."

Jessica patted her hair, which had turned out perfectly in spite of her misgivings about Elizabeth's frame of mind. "Do I look OK? I really want to make a good impression on Mr. Gordon."

"Don't worry," Lila said, "you look fine."

"Fine?" Jessica couldn't conceal her disappointment. "That's it—just fine?"

"OK," Lila conceded with a laugh. "You look unbelievably, fantastically, awesomely ravishing."

"That's better."

Lila whirled about playfully. "Now it's your turn to tell me how ravishing I look."

"Gee, Lila," Jessica teased, "why don't you ask Roger? I'm sure he'd be happy to tell you how gorgeous you look."

They both glanced over at Roger Barrett, who was too busy helping with the scenery to notice.

"He probably dreams about you at night." Jessica closed her eyes and affected a breathy whisper. "Oh, Roger, darling, kiss me, kiss me. . . ."

Lila laughed, "Stop it, Jess! I wouldn't speak to that creep even in his *dreams*, and you know it."

Just then Jessica spotted Bill with his arm around DeeDee. Now it was Lila's turn to tease.

"Looks like the competition has won out. Have you noticed how chummy those two have gotten lately?"

Jessica glanced over and shrugged. "So what?"

"I thought you wanted Bill to be your eternal slave."

"If he'd rather be with DeeDee, let him. She's more his type, anyway. The two of them can sit out in the water on their surfboards until they shrivel up like prunes for all I care."

Lila stared at her friend as if she'd suddenly started speaking a foreign language. "This doesn't sound like the Jessica Wakefield I know. Are you sure you didn't get hit over the head or something on the way over?"

"Let's just say I have more important things on my mind than what Bill and DeeDee are doing."

"Oh, I get it." Lila dropped her voice to a

conspiratorial whisper. "More important, as in movie contract?"

Jessica only smiled mysteriously. Pretty soon it would all be out in the open, and then she could really celebrate. She couldn't wait to see the look on Elizabeth's face when the good news was announced. As far as Bill was concerned, Jessica found it only slightly annoying that he was paying more attention to DeeDee nowadays. Bill was nothing. Soon she would be dating rich movie stars who drove Jaguars and Maseratis. Guys like Bill would be lucky to get her autograph.

"Did you hear about DeeDee coming in third in the surfing championship this morning?" Lila asked.

"Yeah, Cara told me," Jessica replied disinterestedly. She was more absorbed in examining her nail polish.

"Bill was there. He got so excited for her he kissed her in front of everyone. I can't believe Bill would do a thing like that."

"Neither can I, but miracles have been known to happen."

Mr. Jaworski interrupted them to announce it was nearly curtain time. The entire backstage area was in a frenzy. The players were scurrying around, muttering their lines and trying not to bump into the stagehands, who were lugging around props and pieces of scenery. By contrast, Jessica felt fairly calm. Despite the butterflies in her stomach, she was confident DeeDee's father knew true talent when he saw it. She didn't have to try hard; it just shone through naturally.

"Break a leg, Bill," she offered with unusual expansiveness as they took their places onstage. She even felt a little sorry for him. It must be hard for poor Bill to act opposite someone with so much more talent than he.

"Thanks. You, too," he muttered, avoiding her eyes.

He'd been avoiding her a lot this past week, whenever they weren't rehearsing. Under any other circumstances, Jessica would have been livid, but now she was prepared to be forgiving. Even handsome Tom McKay had paled somewhat in comparison to the Warren Beatty types she would soon be linked with. Let Bill have DeeDee, she thought. Those two nerds deserved each other.

Then the curtain was going up, and the auditorium thundered with applause. The lights were hot against her face. Her heart was beating too fast, and her palms felt slippery. But the instant she opened her mouth to say her first lines, her panic was forgotten.

Jessica, the born actress, was in her element.

Elizabeth hugged her sister. "Oh, Jess, you were fantastic! I cried practically the whole way through! It's a good thing Mom brought extra tissues."

"I'll second that," Mr. Wakefield chimed in, stepping over to scoop Jessica into his arms. "Between the two of them, I was afraid they were going to flood the auditorium."

Mrs. Wakefield shot her husband a wry look. "I suppose you'd like us to believe you were sniffling for the last ten minutes because you're coming down with a cold?"

He grinned sheepishly. "I never argue a case when the deck is stacked against me. In this case, I concede. You were truly spellbinding, sweetheart."

"Especially that scene at the end," Elizabeth offered, "when you go looking for Bud and find out he's married to Angelina. It was so sad."

But obviously not for Bill and DeeDee, Elizabeth thought. DeeDee had played the small role of Angelina. It was ironic the way it had all turned out—both onstage and off.

The play had been a huge success. The audience had given Bill and Jessica a standing ovation when it was their turn to take a bow. Jessica just stood there glowing, as if she were used to receiving such adulation. When the stage manager trotted out to thrust a bouquet of roses into her arms, she blew a kiss to the audience. Elizabeth thought the cheers would never stop. She was proud of her sister. She really did hope everything would turn out the way Jessica wanted it to.

DeeDee's father, a tall man with a bushy, blond mustache, was wending his way toward them. He stopped briefly to congratulate Lois Waller, who had played a minor part. She couldn't hear what he was saying, though; there was too much noise. The backstage area had become a madhouse, with the cast members babbling in relief now that it was all over and their friends and family clustering around them to tell them how fantastic they were.

Mr. Gordon came up and shook Jessica's hand. "You gave a fine performance, dear. Keep up the good work."

Then he was gone, swallowed up by the crowd. Jessica blinked in astonishment. There was some kind of huge commotion going on over by Bill Chase. Mr. Gordon was pumping his hand, and Bill wore a dazed, happy look. DeeDee was hugging him. In a loud, excited voice, she cried, "I *knew* it! I just knew it had to be you!"

Jessica refused to believe it. There had to be some mistake. Everyone was congratulating Bill because they wanted to save him from disappointment when Mr. Gordon made the announcement it was *her* he'd picked. Of course, that had to be it. . . .

Lila swooped down on her. "Can you believe it? Bill Chase a movie star? They should put it on 'That's Incredible!' "

But Jessica wasn't listening. She just stood there, gaping at the drama unfolding around Bill, a sense of outrage growing within her. It wasn't fair! She was a million times more talented than Bill. How could they do this to her? How could they

Elizabeth touched her sister's arm, jolting her back to reality. "I'm sorry, Jess. I really am."

Jessica turned on her, eyes glittering with unshed tears. "Say it, why don't you? Say 'I told you so.' "

"Look," Elizabeth said softly, "we all make mistakes. I'm not going to rub your nose in it."

Jessica's mouth narrowed to a hard line. "The only mistake I made was letting that DeeDee get her hooks into Bill. It's all her fault. She probably nagged her father into picking Bill. I'm positive I would have been his first choice if she hadn't gotten in the way."

Recognizing the look in her sister's eyes, Elizabeth said in a low voice, "Don't do it. Leave Bill alone. You've tortured him enough already. Let DeeDee have him now. She really loves him."

Jessica hadn't heard one word. She was already sailing off in Bill and DeeDee's direction, primed for attack.

She was momentarily detoured from her

track, however, by Tom McKay, who had come backstage to see her. "You were great, Jess," he said.

Distracted, Jessica tried to smile. Her thoughts were no longer on Tom. "Oh, uh, thanks."

"Will you be ready to go soon?"

Damn! Jessica thought. In all the excitement she had forgotten she had invited Tom to go with her to the cast party. She had to get out of it somehow. "I don't know how much longer I'll have to hang around here. It may be awhile. Anyway, I can't drive over with you. I had to get here early, so I took the Fiat." She gave Bill her most brilliant smile. "Why don't you just go on ahead? I'll meet you over there."

Tom looked annoyed, but he shrugged and said, "OK. I'll see you there."

Giving Tom one last dazzling smile, Jessica headed toward Bill.

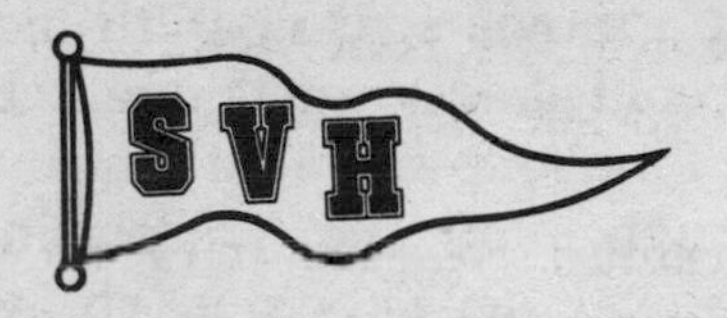

Thirteen

"Congratulations, Bill," Jessica purred. "I just heard the news. It's a funny thing, but I had this feeling all along it was going to be you." She angled herself so that she stood between Bill and DeeDee. Her back was facing DeeDee.

"Thanks, Jessica," Bill said, acknowledging her congratulations with a solemn nod. "But I can't believe this. I never thought Mr. Gordon would single me out."

"Of course, *you* wouldn't think so. That would be conceited, and you're certainly not like that."

The funny part was, Jessica was actually starting to believe the flattery she was heaping on Bill. The edge had worn off her anger, and she was beginning to see him in a new light. He was actually much handsomer than she'd ever realized. Had his eyes always been so blue? She could imagine him blown up a hundred times on a movie screen. With his light blond hair, he could almost be a young Robert Redford.

Yes, Elizabeth was right. She'd tortured him long enough. Now she was playing for keeps. Glancing over her shoulder, she was gratified to see that DeeDee wore a very worried look.

Jessica hooked her arm through Bill's. "You deserved it—more than anybody. Your kind of talent doesn't come along every day." She was glad to see she still had the power to make Bill blush.

"Well, we'll see," he said cautiously. "Mr. Gordon is going to set me up for a couple of screen tests. Until then, nothing's for sure."

"Oh, I just know you'll be great. Someday you're going to be a big star. You might even have your own fan club here at Sweet Valley High."

Bill shifted uncomfortably at the thought of becoming famous. "Yeah, well, like I said, we'll see. Nothing's set. I want to finish school before I make any big decisions about the future."

"If your invitation is still open to take me to the party, we could talk about it some more then," Jessica cooed. "I'm simply *dying* to hear all about your plans. Also, while we're on the subject—what are you doing next Saturday? I thought maybe we could do something to celebrate your success."

Bill didn't say anything. He just stood there, gaping at Jessica in astonishment. He didn't notice when DeeDee slipped away, her eyes glistening with tears. Jessica did, though.

Serves her right, Jessica thought. If it hadn't been for DeeDee's interference, *she* would be having those screen tests instead of Bill.

"Jessica, I can't go to the party with you," Bill said. "I—" He looked around for DeeDee, but she'd disappeared.

Jessica plunged in, saying, "Never mind. I'll meet you there, OK? We can make all our plans then. See you!" She blew him a kiss before whirling off in the opposite direction.

The party was being held at Lila Fowler's estate. Jessica had planned to make a grand entrance—the soon-to-be-superstar. Riding on Bill's glory would be a poor substitute, but it would have to suffice for the moment.

Outside, she breezed past DeeDee, who was sitting on a bench near the darkened gym, her shoulders shaking with quiet sobs. Jessica felt a momentary twinge of pity, which she quickly brushed away.

DeeDee was only getting what she deserved, she reminded herself.

DeeDee didn't know how long she'd been sitting outside. She shivered. It was starting to get chilly, and she'd forgotten to bring a sweater. Oh, well, what difference did it make? Forgetting that it seldom dropped below fifty degrees in Sweet Valley this time of year, she decided she didn't care if she froze to death.

She should have known it was too good to have lasted with Bill. The only reason he'd paid so much attention to her this past week was because Jessica had been ignoring him. Now that Jessica had switched on the charm machine again, DeeDee didn't stand a chance. What had ever made her think she could compete with the dazzling Jessica Wakefield in the first place?

"I know how you feel," a quiet voice said.

Startled, DeeDee looked over to see that Roger Barrett had sat down next to her. Feeling embarrassed, she brushed her wet cheeks with the back of her hand.

"H-how do you know?" she asked.

Roger pulled a clean handkerchief from his pocket and handed it to her. "I may be invisible to most of the kids, but that doesn't mean I'm blind. I've seen the way it is when you're with Bill. I guess you notice stuff like that when you're in the same position."

"What do you mean?" DeeDee stared at Roger in surprise. He'd always seemed so shy and secretive. She couldn't believe he was talking like this.

He shrugged. "Lila and me, in case you haven't already guessed. I know she'd probably laugh in my face if she knew how I felt about her. I'll bet you probably think I'm crazy, too."

"I don't think you're crazy, Roger."

"I guess that's why I'm telling you all this. When you're in the same position as someone, you understand how that person feels."

DeeDee let out a long breath. "For a while I thought I had a chance. I really had myself convinced he'd forgotten about Jessica. But who could forget about Jessica?"

"She's not exactly the invisible type," Roger agreed. "But maybe it's, you know, one of those passing things."

"Maybe," DeeDee said, a bitter note creeping into her voice. "But I'm not going to sit around and wait for anybody. I have my pride."

Roger nodded sympathetically, and she had the feeling he really did understand. DeeDee sat straight, squaring her shoulders. She blew her nose into the tissue that was balled up in her fist.

"Are you going to the party?" she asked him.

"I—I wasn't planning to."

"Why not?"

He paused, staring off into the darkness. Finally he confessed, "I don't have a ride."

"You can ride with me."

"You're going?"

She smiled weakly. "I wasn't planning to, either—until just a minute ago. But I can't go around hiding my head every time something doesn't work out the way I want it to."

Roger remained hesitant. "I don't know,

DeeDee. I feel like such a nothing around Lila. I'm sure nobody wants me there."

"Don't be silly, Roger." DeeDee gave him an unsteady smile as she pushed herself to her feet. "Besides, they say misery loves company. Let's see if it's true."

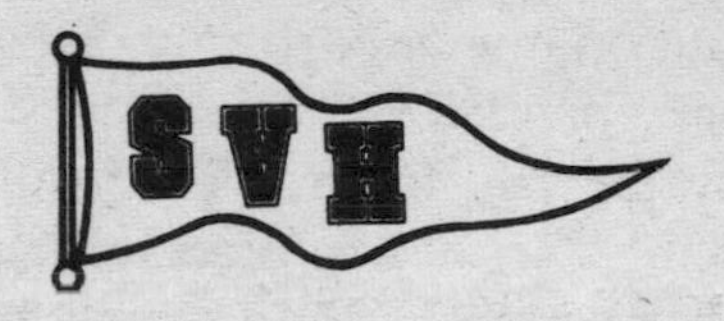

Fourteen

"Forget it, Jess, I'm not going to that party." Elizabeth was sitting on her bed, writing in her journal.

"Come on, Lizzie," Jessica cajoled. "You know I never have as much fun when you're not there. Besides, I *need* you."

"Why don't you get Tom to take you?"

Jessica didn't want to admit that she'd called her date with Tom off at the last minute—now that she had her sights set on Bill.

"Tom and I are finished," she confessed with a little hitch in her voice. Well, at least it *would* be true after that night. "And I should think you'd have a little more sympathy for me after what I've been through." She sniffled once for effect.

"I know how disappointed you are," Elizabeth said, softening. "But look at it this way—you don't have to give up acting just because you lost out on one opportunity. There are bound to be other ones if you keep at it."

"Easy for you to say. You're the one with all the talent," Jessica replied hopelessly.

"Well, I certainly don't expect my first book to be a best seller! I'll be lucky just to get it published. Besides, if you weren't talented, Mr. Jaworski would never have cast you in the lead in the first place."

"He probably did only because he felt sorry for me."

"Come off it, Jess. Don't make me laugh."

"I can't believe how selfish you're being, Liz," Jessica exploded. "Don't you care one bit about my feelings? How do you expect me to face everyone alone after the way I've been humiliated?" Her eyes brimmed with tears.

Elizabeth relented with a sigh. She rose to place a consoling arm about her sister's shoulders. "I do understand. Honestly I do. But I just can't bear the thought of seeing Todd there."

"What's one crummy boyfriend compared to a whole Hollywood career down the tubes?"

"I know it doesn't sound like much to you, but I really loved Todd. I still do, if you want to know the truth."

"Even after what he did to you?"

"I know it sounds weird, but I guess love is like that."

"Well, even so, you can't go on avoiding

him forever. How much longer do you think you can stay home sick from school?"

"That's not fair," Elizabeth protested. "I really *was* sick this week."

True, she thought, it might have been brought on partly by her misery over Todd, but she had been running a low-grade fever. She still felt a little sick to her stomach, too—especially when she thought about Todd and Patsy.

Nonetheless, she recognized the truth in what Jessica was saying. She couldn't go on avoiding Todd forever the way she'd done this week, simply ducking his calls by having her mother say she was too ill to come to the phone. And if Todd and Patsy were in love with each other, she'd better start getting used to the idea, no matter how much it hurt.

"You're not sick anymore," Jessica pointed out impatiently.

"Oh, all right. I'll go." Elizabeth gave a long sigh. Once again, she was bailing her twin out. Once at the party, Elizabeth was sure Jessica would forget all about her, leaving her to deal with Todd alone.

She stood and shook a fist at her sister. "You *really* owe me one for this, Jess!"

Jessica wore her most angelic expression. "Why, Liz, you sound as if I ask for favors all the time."

Elizabeth gave an exasperated groan. She

loved her sister better than anyone, but there were times when she could have cheerfully tossed her into a tank of man-eating sharks.

The Fowler mansion was enormous. Elizabeth couldn't help thinking, as they pulled up in front of it, that three houses the size of the Wakefields' own comfortable split-level could have easily fit into this impressive building.

A uniformed maid ushered the twins into a huge living room carpeted ankle-deep in champagne-colored shag. The party was already in full swing. A bunch of kids were dancing. Elizabeth felt a stab of jealousy as she watched a couple with their arms twined about each other's waist. She and Todd had once danced that way, oblivious to the rest of the world.

"Hi, Liz, I didn't know you were coming!" a girl's voice chirped.

Elizabeth swiveled about, neatly spilling the root beer Jessica had thrust into her hand before rushing off. Patsy! She looked stunning in a low-cut halter-top jumpsuit made of some shimmery, peach-colored fabric.

"Uh, hi," Elizabeth muttered, wishing the floor would open up to swallow her.

"Have you seen Todd?" Patsy asked, seemingly oblivious to Elizabeth's torture. "He said he was going out to get something from his car.

I just thought you might have run into him on your way in."

Elizabeth couldn't believe it. How could anyone be so insensitive? Tears stung her eyes. It had been a mistake to come here after all. Right now, all she wanted to do was escape.

"Excuse me." She pushed past Patsy, heading back toward the front door.

Out of the corner of her eye, she caught a glimpse of Jessica, sitting next to Bill on the couch, working her spell on him. Elizabeth knew she should tell her sister she was leaving, but she didn't think that in her present state she could handle another argument. Besides, knowing her sister, Jessica would have at least a dozen ride offers by the end of the evening.

Outside, Elizabeth stood on the porch and closed her eyes, letting the cool night air wash over her flushed face. Tears spilled out from under her lids. She would never be able to get used to it. She would never be able to look at Todd and Patsy without feeling as if she'd been stabbed in the heart.

Suddenly she jumped as a pair of strong arms closed around her from behind, trapping her arms against her sides.

"It's no use trying to escape." Todd's voice was husky against her ear. "I'm not letting you loose until you tell me what's going on. Liz, are you trying to break up with me or what?"

Elizabeth wrenched about to face him. "*Me—*

trying to break up with *you*?" she choked. "Is that supposed to be some kind of sick joke?"

Todd wasn't smiling. "All I know is that you've been running away from me every time I try to get near you. You didn't return any of my calls this week. I don't understand it, Liz. I feel I've suddenly developed a contagious disease or something."

"You're wasting your time," Elizabeth said coldly. "I know all about you and Patsy."

"Patsy?" Todd looked confused. "What about Patsy and me?"

Elizabeth tried to yank away, but Todd had her firmly in his grasp. In frustration she blurted, "I was looking for you after school one day, and I saw you at your locker with—with your arms around her! And don't you dare deny it!"

"I'm not going to," said Todd quietly. "It's true."

Elizabeth was sobbing openly now. Todd's face had dissolved into a wavery blur. "I h-have to go now, Todd. P-please let me g-go."

"Nothing doing. Not until you've heard the rest of it."

"Please, Todd . . ." Elizabeth struggled weakly against him. "I don't want to hear any more."

"Will you just listen? Patsy was really upset that day. She'd just gotten a letter from her boyfriend in France telling her he'd met someone else. She was really broken up about it, so I put my arms around her to comfort her."

"That's it?" Elizabeth wanted to believe him, she really did.

"That's it. I told you once before, Liz, but I guess you weren't listening. Patsy and I are just friends. You're the one I love." His arms dropped from her waist. "Now, if you still want to run away, I'm not going to try to stop you."

Elizabeth looked hard into his face, at the sincerity shining from his brown eyes. And she knew he was telling the truth. She'd been wrong to doubt him, terribly wrong.

"I don't know what to say," she whispered. "I feel like such a dope."

He smiled crookedly. "Lucky for you I happen to have a soft spot for dopes."

"Oh, Todd . . ."

She snuggled against his chest, breathing in the clean, starchy scent of his freshly ironed shirt. It felt so good to be in his arms. The tears continued to spill down her cheeks, but now they were tears of happiness.

"Hey." Todd tipped her chin up to meet his gaze. His eyes were dark and liquid with emotion. "Don't cry. There's a penalty for crying, you know."

"Oh, yeah? What is it?"

"This." He leaned down and kissed her, setting loose a flurry of warm sensations in her. "And there's more where that came from if you don't watch it."

Elizabeth's laugh ended up a hiccup. "What's the punishment for saying 'I love you'?"

"Oh, that's really heavy-duty. Possible life imprisonment."

He kissed her again, more firmly this time. Elizabeth felt herself melting against him.

"I surrender," she murmured happily.

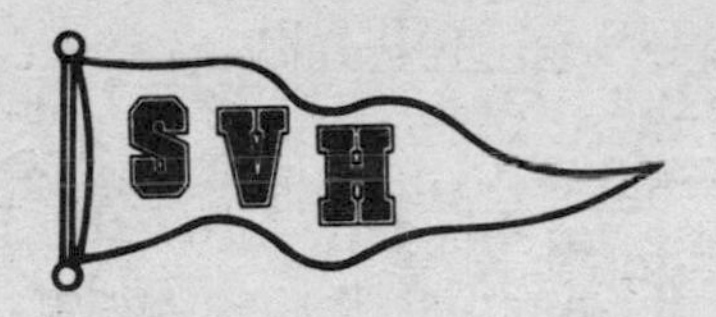

Fifteen

Jessica snuggled closer to Bill on the couch. He seemed strangely ill at ease, she thought. Maybe it was just the effect of her nearness. She smiled at the knowledge that she hadn't lost her power over him.

"I was thinking about our little celebration," she cooed, sliding her arm through his. "Let's make it a barbecue at the beach. The beach is so romantic, don't you think?"

"Jessica, I—"

But Jessica barreled on. "That way you can start teaching me how to surf. Oh, won't that be neat? When I heard how you coached DeeDee into winning third place in the championship, I was really impressed."

"About DeeDee—"

"Oh, you don't have to explain, Bill. I know she's wild about you, poor thing. But, who could blame her? I'll bet there are a million girls who'd like to be with you."

She shot him a coy upward glance through the dark fringe of her lashes. She was practically sitting on his lap. Now she let her head rest daintily against his shoulder, her golden hair spilling down his arm.

Bill stood up so suddenly that Jessica's head was jerked back against the couch. Ginger ale sloshed over the brim of the paper cup he'd been drinking from, sprinkling her bare arm with ice-cold droplets. He was staring past her, a glazed expression on his face. Jessica followed his gaze over to the front door, where DeeDee had just walked in with Roger Barrett.

He probably feels guilty about dumping her, Jessica thought. Too bad. Now that Bill was almost a movie star, she wasn't about to let DeeDee get her net around him again. Not that she really had anything to worry about. No one in his right mind would want DeeDee Gordon when he could have Jessica Wakefield.

"DeeDee!" Bill cried, rushing over to meet her. "What happened? I thought you were coming to the party with me."

DeeDee's cheeks flushed pink, but her smile never wavered. "I could see you were busy," she replied. "I figured you and Jessica would want to be alone to make plans for your celebration on Saturday."

"That was really sweet of you, DeeDee,"

Jessica drawled, rising from the couch and walking over to stand beside Bill.

Ignoring Jessica, Bill grabbed DeeDee's elbow as she moved to turn away. "Wait a minute. I think there's been some kind of misunderstanding here." He glanced over at Jessica. "I've been trying to tell you, I can't make it on Saturday."

"Oh, no problem. We can just as easily do it Sunday. In fact, that might even be better."

"Sunday is out, too." He put his arm around DeeDee, pulling her close as he stared into her eyes. "Same with the weekend after that. You see, Jessica, I'm going to be pretty tied up from now on."

Tied up? Jessica couldn't believe what she was hearing. It wasn't possible! He was telling her he'd rather be with DeeDee.

DeeDee was gazing back at Bill with an ecstatic expression that made Jessica want to throw up. What a nerd! For that matter, Bill was a nerd, too. Those two deserved each other. How could she ever have been so blind as to think she could be in love with Bill? Ugh!

Nevertheless, Jessica couldn't fight the blush that was climbing up the sides of her face. It spread over her cheeks with a throbbing heat. She could feel her ears burning. It was rare for her to blush, but when it happened, it was a major Technicolor event.

With a choked cry, she fled. This was too much! What should have been the best night of her life was rapidly becoming the worst.

"I don't think Jessica was too happy about your turning down her invitation," DeeDee said to Bill after they had strolled outside to the patio to escape the crush of the party.

Bill smiled knowingly. "Oh, she'll survive."

DeeDee glanced up at him shyly. "You're sure, really sure you're not still in love with her?"

That was when he kissed her. It was even better than the other times. Because she knew it was for keeps. It left her heart pounding. Bill cupped her face with gentle hands as he drew back. The pads of his thumbs moved in slow circles over her temples, while his fingers tangled in her dark curls.

DeeDee's pulse skidded out of control. Every sense was singing with life.

His hands slid down over her bare arms, which were rippled with gooseflesh. "Cold?" he asked.

"Just happy." She pressed her cheek against the pleasant wooly scratchiness of his shoulder.

"I hope that answered your question," he murmured against her hair.

"Mmm . . . I'm not sure. I may need a little more convincing."

He drew her to him again in a long, lingering kiss.

"Any better?" he asked.

"Keep it up. This may take all night."

"What about the party?"

"Oh, I'm sure Lila won't mind if we leave early. It's for a good cause."

"Yeah?"

"Well, if you're going to be America's new teen sex symbol, you're going to need a lot of practice acting sexy, right?"

He laughed. "If you say so. Are you applying for the job of coach?"

"Are you accepting applications?"

"Just one."

He lowered his mouth against hers, stopping any further conversation. DeeDee let herself be carried away on a wave of warm sensations. It was an enchanted night, in spite of the way it had started out.

Gently she pulled away and looked up at Bill. The moonlight bleached his hair to silver-white, and his eyes looked almost black. She touched his cheek. There was something she wanted to tell him, but at the moment she was too full of emotion for words.

Bill said it for her. "I know. I love you, too."

Sixteen

"You must be losing your magic touch, Jess," Cara teased. "First Bill, and now Tom. That's two strikes in one night."

Jessica glared at Cara. It was humiliating enough without having her friends making a big joke out of it!

"Bill's a creep," she snapped. "I was getting tired of him, anyway. It's a relief to have DeeDee take him off my hands."

"What about Tom? Did you notice that he and Patsy have been dancing practically every dance together?" She giggled. "Maybe the punch was spiked with Elmer's Glue."

Jessica didn't laugh. In fact, there was nothing even remotely funny about this whole evening as far as she was concerned.

Through the sliding glass door that led out onto the patio, she caught a glimpse of Bill and DeeDee. DeeDee was laughing. Bill bent to smooth a wisp of hair from her cheek and whisper something in her ear. Jessica looked away. She couldn't stand to watch anymore. Those two made her sick.

"What about Roger?" Cara asked cattily. "Look at him—he's been sitting over there in the corner by himself practically the whole evening. I'll bet he could use some company."

Jessica pounced upon it as the perfect chance to divert the conversation away from the painful topic of her failures. With a wicked smile, she turned to Lila, who had just walked up.

"I think we should save Roger for Lila. Don't you think they'd make an adorable couple?"

Lila groaned and clutched at her stomach. "Ugh! Don't make me ill!"

Cara played along with the gag. "I don't know. I think he's kind of cute, Lila."

"Why don't you go over there and ask him to dance?" urged Jessica. "After all, it's your party. You're supposed to make all the guests feel welcome."

Lila was on the verge of turning green. "I wouldn't dance with Roger Barrett if he were the last boy on earth!" she declared.

Unfortunately, just as she said it, the record that had been playing ended. In the lull that followed, Lila's voice carried across the room, every word audible.

It was obvious from the flash flood of red that washed across Roger's cheeks that he'd heard. His eyes glistened. Even at a distance, Jessica could see the painful way his Adam's apple was working above his collar. She couldn't help feeling a little sorry for him.

Even Lila looked embarrassed as Roger twisted out of his chair, bolting from the room as if he'd just discovered it was on fire.

Elizabeth, glowing as she walked in on Todd's arm, was just in time to witness the execution.

"Poor Roger," she said to Todd. "Looks like he's been put up before the Fowler firing squad."

What would Lila do if she ever discovered Roger's secret? she wondered. All her sympathy went out to him. Roger's crush on Lila was worse than hopeless. It was positively heartrending.

(*Roger and Lila have big surprises in store for them in Sweet Valley High #9,* LOVE ON THE RUN.)